"Julie." He repeated her name and she stopped dead.

She might have known he'd come.

Dear heaven, he was beautiful. He was tall, almost lanky, still boyish even though he must be—what?—thirty-six by now?

He had the same blond-brown hair that looked perpetually as if he spent too much time in the sun. He had the same flop of cowlick that perpetually hung a bit too long—no hairdresser believed it wouldn't stay where it was put. He was wearing his normal casual clothes: moleskins, with a soft linen shirt rolled up at the sleeves and open at the throat.

He was wearing the same smile in the caramel-brown eyes she remembered. He was smiling at her now. A bit wary. Not sure of his reception.

She hadn't seen him for four years and he was wary. She didn't know where to start. Where to begin after all this time.

Why not say it like it was?

"I don't think I *am* Julie," she said slowly, feeling lost. "At least, I'm not sure I'm the Julie you know."

Dear Reader,

I've always dreamed of a white Christmas, of snow outside and bright fires within. I've thought longingly of weather in which roast turkey and plum pudding are truly, mouthwateringly appropriate. But of course I live in Australia, where plum pudding is often made with ice cream—because who can bear to turn on the stove?

And sometimes the fires are burning outside.

For Christmas in Australia is bushfire season. In the Australian bush we celebrate with a wary eye on the weather maps and with our fire plans made.

Christmas joy, though, seems to catch up with us wherever we are, and while I've been writing this book that's what I've been remembering. Christmas isn't about the weather or the food. It's about love and it's about joy.

In my book, Julie and Rob have lost their way through tragedy. They've lost their love and their joy. It takes a thoroughly Australian bushfire—and a truly Australian Christmas—to teach them what really matters. At Christmas, they're where they belong.

I wish the same for you.

Marion

Christmas Where They Belong

Marion Lennox

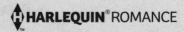

HARLEQUIN® ROMANCE

Recycling programs
for this product may
not exist in your area.

ISBN-13: 978-0-373-74317-9

Christmas Where They Belong

First North American Publication 2014

Copyright © 2014 by Marion Lennox

Printed in U.S.A.

Marion Lennox is a country girl, born on an Australian dairy farm. She moved on—mostly because the cows just weren't interested in her stories! Married to a "very special doctor," Marion also writes for the Harlequin Medical Romance™ line. (She used a different name for each category for a while—readers looking for her past Harlequin Romance titles should search for author Trisha David, as well.) She's now had more than seventy-five romance novels accepted for publication.

In her non-writing life Marion cares for kids, cats, dogs, chooks and goldfish. She travels, and she fights her rampant garden (she's losing) and her house dust (she's lost). Having spun in circles for the first part of her life, she's now stepped back from her "other" career, which was teaching statistics at her local university. Finally she's reprioritized her life, figured out what's important and discovered the joys of deep baths, romance and chocolate. Preferably all at the same time!

Recent books by Marion Lennox

This and other titles by Marion Lennox are also available in ebook format from www.Harlequin.com.

This book is dedicated to Lorna May Dickins.

Her kindness, her humor and her love are an
inspiration for always.

CHAPTER ONE

'DIDN'T YOU ONCE own a house in the Blue Mountains?'

'Um…yes.'

'Crikey, Jules, you wouldn't want to be there now. The whole range looks about to burn.'

It was two days before Christmas. The Australian world of finance shut down between Christmas and New Year, but the deal Julie McDowell was working on was international. The legal issues were urgent.

But the Blue Mountains… Fire.

She dumped her armload of contracts and headed for Chris's desk. At thirty-two, Chris was the same age as Julie, but her colleague's work ethic was as different from hers as it was possible to be. Chris worked from nine to five and not a moment more before he was off home to his wife and kids in the suburbs. Sometimes he even surfed the Web during business hours.

Sure enough, his computer was open at the

Web browser now. She came up behind him and saw a fire map. The Blue Mountains. A line of red asterisks.

Her focus went straight to Mount Bundoon, a tiny hamlet right in the centre of the asterisks. The hamlet she'd once lived in.

'Is it on fire?' she gasped. She'd been so busy she hadn't been near a news broadcast for hours. Days?

'Not yet.' Chris zoomed in on a few of the asterisks. 'These are alerts, not evacuation orders. A storm came through last night, with lighting strikes but not much rain. The bush is tinder dry after the drought, and most of these asterisks show spot fires in inaccessible bushland. But strong winds and high temperatures are forecast for tomorrow. They're already closing roads, saying she could be a killer.'

A killer.

The Blue Mountains.

You wouldn't want to be there now.

She went back to her desk and pulled up the next contract. This was important. She needed to concentrate, but the words blurred before her eyes. All she could see was a house—long, low, every detail architecturally designed, built to withstand the fiercest bush fires.

In her mind she walked through the empty house to a bedroom with two small beds in the shape of racing cars. Teddies sitting against the pillows. Toys. A wall-hanging of a steam train her mother had made.

She hadn't been there for four years. It should have been sold. Why hadn't it?

She fought to keep her mind on her work. This had to be dealt with before Christmas.

Teddies. A wardrobe full of small boys' clothes.

She closed her eyes and she was there again, tucking two little boys into bed, watching Rob read them their bedtime story.

It was history, long past, but she couldn't open her eyes. She couldn't.

'Julie? Are you okay?' Her boss was standing over her, sounding concerned. Bob Marsh was a financial wizard but he looked after his staff, especially those who brought as much business to the firm as Julie.

She forced herself to open her eyes and tried for a smile. It didn't work.

'What's up?'

'The fire.' She took a deep breath, knowing what she was facing. Knowing she had no choice.

'I *do* have a house in the Blue Mountains,' she managed. 'If it's going to burn there are things I need to save.' She gathered her pile of contracts and did what she'd never done in all her years working for Opal, Harbison and Marsh. She handed the pile to Bob. 'You'll need to deal with this,' she told him. 'I'm sorry, but…'

She couldn't finish the sentence. She grabbed her purse and went.

Rob McDowell was watching the fire's progress on his phone. He'd downloaded an app to track it by, and he'd been checking it on and off for hours.

He was in Adelaide, working. His clients had wanted to be in the house by Christmas and he'd bent over backwards to make it happen. Their house was brilliant and there were only a few decorative touches left to be made. Rob was no longer needed, but Sir Cliff and Lady Claudia had requested their architect to stay on until tomorrow.

He should. They were having a housewarming on Christmas Eve, and socialising at the end of a job was important. The *Who's Who* of Adelaide, maybe even the *Who's Who* of the entire country would be here. There weren't many people who could beckon the cream of society on Christmas Eve but Sir Cliff and Lady Claudia had that power. As the architect of their stunning home, Rob could expect scores of professional approaches afterwards.

But it wasn't just professional need that

was driving him. For the last few years he'd flown overseas to the ski fields for Christmas but somehow this year they'd lost their appeal. Christmas had been a nightmare for years but finally he was beginning to accept that running away didn't help. He might as well stay for the party, he'd decided, but now he checked the phone app again and felt worse. The house he and Julie had built was right in the line of fire.

The house would be safe, he told himself. He'd designed it himself and it had been built with fires like this one in mind.

But no house could withstand the worst of Australia's bush fires. He knew that. To make its occupants safe he'd built a bunker into the hill behind the house, but the house itself could go up in flames.

It was insured. No one was living there. It shouldn't matter.

But the contents…

The contents.

He should have cleared it out by now, he thought savagely. He shouldn't have left everything there. The tricycles. The two red fire engines he'd chosen himself that last Christmas.

Julie might have taken them.

She hadn't. She would have told him.

Both of them had walked away from their

house four years ago. It should have been on the market, but…but…

But he'd paid a housekeeping service to clean it once a month, and to clear the grounds. He was learning to move on, but selling the house, taking this last step, still seemed…too hard.

So what state was it in now? he wondered. Had the bushland encroached again? If there was bushland growing against the house…

It didn't matter. The house was insured, he told himself again. What did it matter if it burned? Wouldn't that just be the final step in moving on with his life?

But two fire engines…

This was ridiculous. He was thinking of forgoing the social event of the season, a career-building triumph, steps to the future, to save two toy fire engines?

But…

'Sarah…' He didn't know what he intended to say until the words were in his mouth, but the moment he said it he knew his decision was right.

'Yeah?' The interior decorator was balancing on a ladder, her arms full of crimson tulle. The enormous drawing room was going to look stunning. 'Could you hand me those ribbons?'

'I can't, Sarah,' he said, in a voice he scarcely recognised. 'I own a house in the Blue Mountains and they're saying the fire threat's getting worse. Could you make my excuses? I need to go…home.'

At the headquarters of the Blue Mountains Fire Service, things looked grim and were about to get worse. Every time a report came in, more asterisks appeared on the map. The fire chief had been staring at it for most of the day, watching spot fires erupt, while the weather forecast grew more and more forbidding.

'We won't be able to contain this,' he eventually said, heavily. 'It's going to break out.'

'Evacuate?' His second-in-command was looking even more worried than he was.

'If we get one worse report from the weather guys, yes. We'll put out a pre-evacuation warning tonight. Anyone not prepared to stay and firefight should leave now.' He looked again at the map and raked his thinning hair. 'Okay, people, let's put the next step of fire warnings into place. Like it or not, we're about to mess with a whole lot of people's Christmases.'

CHAPTER TWO

THE HOUSE LOOKED just as she'd left it. The garden had grown, of course. A couple of trees had grown up close to the house. Rob wouldn't be pleased. He'd say it was a fire risk.

It was a fire risk.

She was sitting in the driveway in her little red coupé, staring at the front door. Searching for the courage to go inside.

It was three years, eleven months, ten days since she'd been here.

Rob had brought her home from hospital. She'd wandered into the empty house; she'd looked around and it was almost as if the walls were taunting her.

You're here and they're not. What sort of parents are you? What sort of parents were you?

She hadn't even stayed the night. She couldn't. She'd thrown what she most needed into a suitcase and told Rob to take her to a hotel.

'Julie, we can do this.' She still heard Rob's

voice; she still saw his face. 'We can face this together.'

'It wasn't you who slept while they died.' She'd thrown that at him, he hadn't answered and she'd known right then that the final link had snapped.

She hadn't been back since.

Go in, she told herself now. *Get this over.*

She opened the car door and the heat hit her with such force that she gasped.

It was dusk. It shouldn't be this hot, this late.

The tiny hamlet of Mount Bundoon had looked almost deserted as she'd driven through. Low-lying smoke and the lack of wind was giving it a weird, eerie feeling. She'd stopped at the general store and bought milk and bread and butter, and the lady had been surprised to see her.

'We're about to close, love,' she said. 'Most people are packing to get out or have already left. You're not evacuating?'

'The latest warning is watch and wait.'

'They've upgraded it. Unless you plan on defending your home, they're advising you get out, if not now, then at least by nine in the morning. That's when the wind's due to rise, but most residents have chosen to leave straight away.'

Julie had hesitated at that. The road up here had been packed with laden cars, trailers, horse floats, all the accoutrements people treasured. That was why she was here. To take things she treasured.

But now she thought: *it wasn't*. She sat in the driveway and stared at the house where she'd once lived, and she thought, even though the house was full of the boys' belongings, it wasn't possessions she wanted.

Was it just to be here? One last time?

It wasn't going to burn, she told herself. It'd still be here…for ever. But that was a dumb thought. They'd have to sell eventually.

That'd mean contacting Rob.

Don't go there.

Go in, she told herself. *Hunker down. This house is fire-safe. In the morning you can walk away but just for tonight… Just for tonight you can let yourself remember.*

Even if it hurt so much it nearly killed her.

Eleven o'clock. The plane had been delayed, because of smoke haze surrounding Sydney. 'There's quite a fire down there, ladies and gentlemen,' the pilot had said as they skirted the Blue Mountains. 'Just be thankful you're up here and not down there.'

But he'd wanted to be down there. By the time he'd landed the fire warnings for Mount Bundoon had been upgraded. *Leave if safe to do so*. Still, the weather forecast was saying the winds weren't likely to pick up until early morning. Right now there was little wind. The house would be safe.

So he'd hired a car and driven into the mountains, along roads where most of the traffic was going in the other direction. When he'd reached the outskirts of Mount Bundoon he'd hit a road block.

'Your business, sir?' he was asked.

'I live here.' How true was that? He didn't live anywhere, he conceded, but maybe here was still…home. 'I just need to check all my fire prevention measures are in place and operational.'

'You're aware of the warnings?'

'I am, but my house is pretty much fire-safe and I'll be out first thing in the morning.'

'You're not planning on defending?'

'Not my style.'

'Not mine either,' the cop said. 'They're saying the wind'll be up by nine, turning to the north-west, bringing the fire straight down here. The smoke's already making the road hazardous. We're about to close it now, allowing no one else in. I shouldn't let you pass.'

'I'll be safe. I'm on my own and I'll be in and out in no time.'

'Be out by the time the wind changes, if not before,' he said grudgingly.

'I will be.'

'Goodnight, then, sir,' the cop said. 'Stay safe.'

'Same to you, in spades.'

He drove on. The smoke wasn't thick, just a haze like a winter fog. The house was on the other side of town, tucked into a valley overlooking the Bundoon Creek. The ridges would be the most dangerous places, Rob thought, not the valley. He and Julie had thought about bush fire when they'd built. If you were planning to build in the Australian bush, you were stupid if you didn't.

Maybe they'd been stupid anyway. Building so far out of town. Maybe that was why…

No. Don't think why. That was the way of madness.

Nearly home. That was a dumb thing to think, too, but he turned the last bend and thought of all the times he'd come home, with kids, noise, chaos, all the stuff associated with twins. Sometimes he and Julie would manage the trip back together and that was the best. *'Mummy, Daddy—you're both here…'*

Cut it out, he told himself fiercely. *You were dumb to come. Don't make it any worse by thinking of the past.*

But the past was all around him, even if it was shrouded in smoke.

'I'll take their toys and get out of here,' he

told himself, and then he pulled into the driveway… and the lights were on.

She'd turned on all the lights to scare the ghosts.

No. If there were any ghosts here she'd welcome them with open arms—it wasn't ghosts she was scared of. It was the dark. It was trying to sleep in this house, and remembering.

She lay on the king-sized bed she and Rob had bought the week before their wedding and she knew sleep was out of the question. She should leave.

But leaving seemed wrong, too. Not when the kids were here.

The kids weren't here. Only memories of them.

This was crazy. She was a legal financier, a good one, specialising in international monetary negotiations. No one messed with her. No one questioned her sanity.

So why was she lying in bed hoping for ghosts?

She lay completely still, listening to the small sounds of the night. The scratching of a possum in the tree outside the window. A night owl calling.

This house had never been quiet. She found herself aching for noise, for voices, for…something.

She got something. She heard a car pull into the driveway. She saw the glimmer of headlights through the window.

The front door opened, and she knew part of her past had just returned. The ghost she was most afraid of.

'Julie?' He'd guessed it must be her before he even opened the door. Firstly the car. It was a single woman's car, expensive, a display of status.

Rob normally drove a Land Rover. Okay, maybe that was a status thing as well, he conceded. He liked the idea that he might spend a lot of time on rural properties but in truth most of his clients were city based. But still, he couldn't drive a car like the one in the driveway. No one here could. No one who commuted from here to the city. No one who taxied kids.

Every light was on in the house. Warning off ghosts?

It had to be Julie.

If she was here the last thing he wanted was to scare her, so the moment he opened the door he called, 'Julie, are you here? It's Rob.'

And she emerged from their bedroom.

Julie.

The sight of her made him feel… No. He couldn't begin to define how he felt seeing her.

It had been nearly four years. She'd refused to see him since.

'I slept while they died and I can't forgive myself. Ever. I can't even think about what I've lost. If I hadn't slept...'

She'd thrown it at him the day he'd brought her home from hospital. He'd spent weeks sick with self-blame, sick with emptiness, not knowing how to cope with his own grief, much less hers. The thought that she blamed herself hadn't even occurred to him. It should have, but in those crucial seconds after she'd said it he hadn't had a response. He'd stared at her, numb with shock and grief, as she'd limped into the bedroom on her crutches, thrown things into a suitcase and demanded he take her to a hotel.

And that had pretty much been that. One marriage, one family, finished.

He'd written to her. Of course he had, and he'd tried to phone. *'Jules, it was no one's fault. That you were asleep didn't make any difference. I was awake and alert. The landslip came from nowhere. There's nothing anyone can do when the road gives way.'* Did he believe it himself? He tried to. Sometimes he had flashes when he almost did.

And apparently, Julie had shared his doubts. She'd written back, brief and harsh.

I was asleep when my babies died. I wasn't there for them, or for you. I can barely live with myself, much less face you every day for the rest of my life. I'm sorry, Rob, but however we manage to face the future, we need to do it alone.

And he couldn't help her to forgive herself. He was too busy living with his *own* guilt. The mountain road to the house had been eroded by heavy spring rains and the collapse was catastrophic. They'd spent the weeks before Christmas in the city apartment because there'd been so much on it had just been too hard to commute. They were exhausted but Julie had been desperate to get up to the mountains for the weekend before Christmas, to make everything perfect for the next week. To let the twins set up their Christmas tree. So Santa wouldn't find one speck of dust, one thing out of place.

He'd gone along with it. Maybe he'd also agreed. Perfection was in both their blood; they were driven personalities. They'd given their nanny the weekend off and they'd driven up here late.

But if they'd just relaxed... If they'd simply said there wasn't time, they could have spent that last weekend playing with the boys in the city, just stopping. But stopping wasn't in their vocabulary and the boys were dead because of it.

Enough. The past needed to be put aside. Julie was standing in their bedroom door.

She looked…beautiful.

He'd thought this woman was gorgeous the moment he'd met her. Tall, willow-slim, blonde hair with just a touch of curl, brown eyes a man could drown in, lips a man wanted to taste…

It was four years since he'd last seen her, and she was just the same but…tighter. It was like her skin was stretched to fit. She was thinner. Paler. She was wearing a simple cotton nightgown, her hair was tousled and her eyes were wide with…wariness.

Why should she be wary of him?

'Julie.' He repeated her name and she stopped dead.

She might have known he'd come.

Dear heaven, he was beautiful. He was tall—she'd forgotten how tall—and still boyish, even though he must be—what, thirty-six?—by now.

He had the same blond-brown hair that looked perpetually like he spent too much time in the sun. He had the same flop of cowlick that hung a bit too long—no hairdresser believed it wouldn't stay where it was put. He was wearing his casual clothes, clothes he might have worn four years ago: moleskins with a soft linen shirt, rolled up at the sleeves and open at the throat.

He was wearing the same smile, a smile which reached the caramel-brown eyes she remembered. He was smiling at her now. A bit hesitant. Not sure of his reception.

She hadn't seen him for four years and he was wary. What did he think she'd do, throw him out?

But she didn't know where to start. Where to begin after all this time.

Why not say it like it was?

'I don't think I am Julie,' she said slowly, feeling lost. 'At least, I'm not sure I'm the Julie you know.'

There was a moment's pause. He'd figure it out, or she hoped he would. She couldn't go straight back to the point where they'd left off. *How are you, Rob? How have you coped with the last four years?*

The void of four long years made her feel ill.

But he got it. There was a moment's silence and then his smile changed a little. She knew that smile. It reflected his intelligence, his appreciation of a problem. If there was a puzzle, Rob dived straight in. Somehow she'd set him one and he had it sorted.

'Then I'm probably not the guy you know, either,' he told her. 'So can we start from the beginning? Allow me to introduce myself. I'm Rob McDowell, architect, based in Adelaide. I have an interest in this house, ma'am, and the contents. I'm here to put the most…put a few things of special value in a secure place. And you?'

She could do this. She felt herself relax, just a little, and she even managed to smile back.

'Julie McDowell. Legal financier from Sydney. I, too, have an interest in this house.'

'McDowell?' He was caught. 'You still use…'

'It was too much trouble to change it back,' she said and he knew she was having trouble keeping her voice light.

'You're staying despite the fire warnings?'

'The wind's not due to get up until tomorrow morning. I'll be gone at dawn.'

'You've just arrived?'

'Yes.'

'You don't want to take what you want and go?'

'I don't know what I want.' She hesitated. 'I think…there's a wall-hanging… But it seems wrong to just…leave.'

'I had two fire engines in mind,' he admitted. 'But I feel the same.'

'So you'll stay until ordered out?'

'If it doesn't get any worse, maybe I can clear any debris, check the pumps and sprinkler system, fill the spouts, keep any stray spark from catching. At first light I'll go right round the house and eliminate every fire risk I can. I can't do it now. It's too dark. For the sake of a few hours, I'll stay. I don't want this place to burn.'

Why? she wanted to say. *What does this house mean to you?*

What did it mean to her? A time capsule? Maybe it was. This house was what it was like when…

But *when* was unthinkable. And if Rob was here, then surely she could go.

But she couldn't. The threat was still here, even if she wasn't quite sure what was being threatened.

'If you need to stay,' she ventured, 'there's a guest room.'

'Excellent.' They were like two wary dogs, circling each other, she thought. But they'd started this sort of game. She could do this.

'Would you like supper?'

'I don't want to keep you up.'

'I wasn't sleeping. The pantry's stocked and the freezer's full. Things may well be slightly out of date…'

'Slightly!'

'But I'm not dictated to by use-by dates,' she continued. 'I have fresh milk and bread. For anything else, I'm game if you are.'

His brown eyes creased a little, amused. 'A risk-taker, Jules?'

'No!'

'Sorry.' Jules was a nickname and that was against the rules. He realised it and backtracked. 'I meant: have you tried any of the food?'

'I haven't tried,' she conceded.

'You came and went straight to bed?'

'I...yes.'

'Then maybe we both need supper.' He checked his watch. 'It's almost too late for a midnight feast but I could eat two horses. Maybe we could get to know each other over a meal? If you dare, that is?'

And she gazed at him for a long moment and came to a decision.

'I dare,' she said. 'Why not?'

He put the cars in the garage and then they checked the fire situation. 'We'd be fools not to,' Rob said as they headed out to the back veranda to see what they could see.

They could see nothing. The whole valley seemed to be shrouded in smoke. It blocked the moon and the stars. It seemed ominous but there was no glow from any fire. 'And the smoke would be thicker if it was closer,' Rob decreed. 'We're safe enough for now.'

'There are branches overhanging the house.'

'I saw them as I came in but there's no way I'm using a chainsaw in the dark.'

'There's no way you're using a chainsaw,' she snapped and he grinned.

'Don't you trust me?'

'Do I trust any man with a chainsaw? No.'

He grinned, that same smile… *Dear heaven, that smile…*

Play the game. For tonight, she did *not* know this man.

'We have neighbours,' Rob said, motioning to a light in the house next door.

'I saw a child in the window earlier, just as it was getting dark.'

'A child… They should have evacuated.'

'Maybe they still think there's time. There should still be time.'

'Let me check again.' He flicked to the fire app on his phone. 'Same warnings. Evacuate by nine if you haven't already done so. Unless you're planning on staying to defend.'

'Would you?' she asked diffidently. 'Stay and defend?'

'I'd have to be trustworthy with a chainsaw to do that.'

'And are you?' The Rob she knew couldn't be trusted within twenty paces of a power tool.

'No,' he admitted and she was forced to smile

back. Same Rob, then. Same, but different? The Rob of *after*.

This was weird. She should be dressed, she decided, as she padded barefoot back to the kitchen behind him. If he really was a stranger...

He really is a stranger, she told herself. Power tool knowledge or not, four years was a lifetime.

'Right.' In the kitchen, he was all efficiency. 'Food.' He pushed his sleeves high over his elbows and looked as if he meant business. 'I'd kill for a steak. What do you suppose the freezer holds?'

'Who knows what's buried in there?'

'Want to help me find out?'

'Men do the hunting.'

'And women do the cooking?' He had the chest freezer open and was delving among the labelled packages. 'Julie, Julie, Julie. How out of the ark is that?'

'I can microwave a mean TV dinner.'

'Ugh.'

But Rob did cook. She remembered him enjoying cooking. Not often because they'd been far too busy for almost everything domestic but when she'd first met him he'd cooked her some awesome meals.

She'd tried to return the favour, but had only cooked disasters.

'What sort of people occupied this planet?'

Rob was demanding answers from the depths of the freezer. 'Packets, packets and packets. Someone here likes Diet Cuisine. Liked,' he amended. 'Use-by dates of three years ago.'

She used to eat them when Rob was away. She'd cooked for the boys, or their nanny had, but Diet Cuisine was her go-to.

'There must be something more...' He was hauling out packet after packet, tossing them onto the floor behind him. She was starting to feel mortified. Her fault again?

'You'll need to put that stuff back or it'll turn into stinking sog,' she warned.

'Of course.' His voice was muffled. 'So in a thousand years an archaeological dig can find Diet Cuisine and think we were all nuts. And stinking sog? For a stink it'd have to contain substance. Two servings of veggies and four freezer-burned cubes of diced meat do not substance make. But hey, here's a whole beef fillet.' He emerged, waving his find in triumph. 'This is seriously thick. I'm hoping freezer burn might only go halfway in or less. I can thaw it in the microwave, chop off the burn and produce steak fit for a king. I hope. Hang on a minute.'

Fascinated, she watched as he grabbed a torch from the pantry and headed for the back door. That was a flaw in this mock play; he shouldn't have known where a torch was. But in two minutes he was back, brandishing a handful of greens.

'Chives,' he said triumphantly and then glanced dubiously at the enormous green fronds. 'Or they might have been chives some time ago. These guys are mutant onions.'

Clarissa had planted vegetables, she remembered. Their last nanny...

But Rob was taking all her attention. The Rob of now.

She'd expected...

Actually, she hadn't expected. She'd thought she'd never see this man again. She'd vaguely thought she'd be served with divorce papers at some stage, but she hadn't had the courage or the impetus to organise it herself. To have him here now, slicing steak, washing dirt from mutant chives, took a bit of getting used to.

'You do want some?' he asked and she thought *no*. And then she thought: *when did I last eat?*

If he had been a stranger she'd eat with him.

'Yes, please,' she said and was inordinately pleased with herself for getting the words out.

So they ate. The condiments in the pantry still seemed fine, though Rob dared to tackle the bottled horseradish and she wasn't game. He'd fried hunks of bread in the pan juices. They ate steak and chives and fried bread, washed down by mugs of milky tea. All were accompanied by Rob's small talk. He really did act as if they were strangers, thrust together by chance.

Wasn't that the truth?

'So, Julie,' he said finally, as he washed and she wiped. There was a dishwasher but, as neither intended sticking round past breakfast, it wasn't worth the effort. 'If you're planning on leaving at dawn, what would you like to do now? You were sleeping when I got here?'

'Trying to sleep.'

'It doesn't come on demand,' he said, and she caught an edge to his voice that said he lay awake, as she did. 'But you can try. I'll keep watch.'

'What—stand sentry in case the fire comes?'

'Something like that.'

'It won't come until morning.'

'I don't trust forecasts. I'll stay on the veranda with the radio. Snooze a little.'

'I won't sleep.'

'So…you want to join me on fire watch?'

'I…okay.'

'You might want to put something on besides your nightie.'

'What's wrong with the nightie? It's sensible.'

'It's not sensible.'

'It's light.'

'Jules,' he said, and suddenly there was strain in his voice. 'Julie. I know we don't know each other very well. I know we're practically strangers, but there is only a settee on the veranda, and if you sit there looking like that…'

She caught her breath and the play-acting stopped, just like that. She stared at him in disbelief.

'You can't…want me.'

'I've never stopped wanting you,' he said simply. 'I've tried every way I know, but it's not working. Just because we destroyed ourselves… Just because we gave away the idea of family for the rest of our lives, it doesn't stop the wanting. Not everything ended the night our boys died, Julie, though sometimes…often…I wish it had.'

'You still feel…'

'I have no idea what I feel,' he told her. 'I've been trying my best to move on. My shrink says I need to put it all in the background, like a book I can open at leisure and close again when it gets too hard to read. But, for now, all I know is that your nightie is way too skimpy and your eyes are too big and your hair is too tousled and our bed is too close. So I suggest you either head to the bedroom and close the door or go get some clothes on. Because what I want has nothing to do with reality, and everything to do with ghosts. Shrink's advice or not, I can't close the book. Go and get dressed, Julie. Please.'

She stared at him for a long moment. Rob. Her husband.

Her ex-husband. Her ex-life.

She'd closed the door on him four years ago. If she was to survive, that door had to stay firmly closed. Behind that door were emotions she couldn't handle.

She turned away and headed inside. Away from him. Away from the way he tugged her heart.

He sat out on the veranda, thinking he might have scared her right off. She didn't emerge.

Well, what was new? He'd watched the way she'd closed down after the boys' deaths. He was struggling to get free of those emotions but it seemed Julie was holding them close. Behind locked doors.

That was her right.

He sat for an hour and watched the night close in around him. The heat seemed to be getting more oppressive. The smoke hung low over everything, black and thick and stinking of burned forest, threatening enough all by itself, even without flames.

It's because there's no wind, he told himself. Without wind, smoke could hang around for weeks. There was no telling how close the fire was. There was no telling what the risks were if the wind got up.

He should leave. He should make Julie leave, but then… But then…

Her decision to come had been hers alone. She had the right to stay. He wasn't sure what he was protecting, but sitting out on the veranda, with Julie in the house behind him, felt okay. He wasn't sure why, but he did know that, at some level, the decision to come had been the right one.

Maybe it was stupid, he conceded, but maybe they both needed this night. Maybe they both needed to stand sentinel over a piece of their past that needed to be put aside.

And it really did need to be put aside. He'd watched Julie's face when he'd confessed that he wanted her and he'd seen the absolute denial. Even if she was ever to want him again, he'd known then that she wouldn't admit it.

Families were for the past.

He sat on. A light was still on next door. Once he saw a woman walk past the lighted window. Pregnant? Was she keeping the same vigil he was keeping?

If he had kids, he'd have them out of here by now. Hopefully, his neighbour had her car packed and would be gone at dawn, taking her family with her.

Just as he and Julie would be gone at dawn, too.

The moments ticked on. He checked the fire app again. No change.

There were sounds coming from indoors. Suddenly he was conscious of Christmas music. Carols, tinkling out on…a music box?

He remembered that box. It had belonged to one of his aunts. It was a box full of Santa and his elves. You wound the key, opened the box and they all danced.

That box…

Memories were all around him. Childhood Christmases. The day his aunt had given it to them—the Christmas Julie was pregnant. 'It needs a family,' his aunt had said. 'I'd love you to have it.'

His aunt was still going strong. He should give the box back to her, he thought, but meanwhile… Meanwhile, he headed in and Julie was sitting in the middle of the living room floor, attaching baubles to a Christmas tree. She was still dressed in the nightgown. She was totally intent on what she was doing.

What…?

'It's Christmas Eve tomorrow,' she said simply, as if this was a no-brainer. 'This should be up. And don't look at the nightgown, Rob Mc-

Dowell. Get over it. It's hot, my nightie's cool and I'm working.'

She'd hauled the artificial tree from the store-room. He stared at it, remembering the Christmas when they'd conceded getting a real tree was too much hassle. It'd take hours to buy it and set it up, and one thing neither of them had was hours.

That last Christmas, that last weekend, the tree was one of the reasons they'd come up here.

'We can decorate the tree for Christmas,' Julie had said. 'When we go up next week we can walk straight in and it'll be Santa-ready.'

Now Julie was sitting under the tree, sorting decorations as if she had all the time in the world. As if nothing had happened. As if time had simply skipped a few years.

'Remember this one?' She held up a very tubby angel with floppy, sparkly wings and a cute little halo. 'I bought this the year I was trying to diet. Every time I looked at a mince pie I was supposed to march in here and discuss it with my angel. It didn't work. She'd look straight back at me and say: "Look at me—I might be tubby but not only am I cute, I grew wings. Go ahead and eat."'

He grinned, recognising the cute little angel with affection.

'And these.' Smiling fondly, he knelt among

the ornaments and produced three reindeer, one slightly chewed. 'We had six of these. Boris ate the other three.'

'And threw them up when your partners came for Christmas drinks.'

'Not a good moment. I miss Boris.' He'd had Boris the Bloodhound well before they were married. He'd died of old age just before the twins were born. Before memories had to be put aside.

They'd never had time for another dog. Maybe now they never would?

Forget it. Bauble therapy. Julie had obviously immersed herself in it and maybe he could, too. He started looping tinsel around the tree and found it oddly soothing.

They worked in silence but the silence wasn't strained. It was strangely okay. Come dawn they'd walk away from this house. Maybe it would burn, but somehow, however strange, the idea that it'd burn looking lived in was comforting.

'How long do Christmas puddings last?' Julie asked at last, as she hung odd little angels made of spray-painted macaroni. Carefully not mentioning who'd made them. The twins with their nanny. The twins…

Concentrate on pudding, he told himself. Concentrate on the practical. *How long do Christmas puddings last?* 'I have no idea,' he conceded. 'I know fruitcakes are supposed to last for ever. My great-grandma cooked them for her brothers during the War. Great-Uncle Henry once told me he used to chop 'em up and lob 'em over to the enemy side. Grandma Ethel's cakes were never great at the best of times but after a few months on the Western Front they could have been lethal.'

'Death by fruitcake…'

'Do you remember the Temperance song?' he asked, grinning at another memory. His great-aunt's singing. He raised his voice and tried it out. *'We never eat fruitcake because it has rum. And one little bite turns a man to a…'*

'Yeah, right.' She smiled back at him and he felt strangely triumphant.

Why did it feel so important to make this woman smile?

Because he'd lost her smile along with everything else? Because he'd loved her smile?

'Clarissa made one that's still in the fridge,' she told him. Nanny Clarissa had been so domestic she'd made up for both of them. Or almost. 'And it does contain rum. Half a bottle of over-proof, if I remember. She demanded I put it on the shopping list that last… Anyway, I'm thinking of frying slices for breakfast.'

'Breakfast is what…' he checked his watch

'...three hours away? Four-year-old Christmas pudding. That'll be living on the edge.'

'A risk worth taking?' she said tightly and went back to bauble-hanging. 'What's to lose?'

'Pudding at dawn. Bring it on.'

They worked on. There were so many tensions zooming round the room. So many things unsaid. All they could do was concentrate on the tree.

Finished, it looked magnificent. They stood back, Rob flicked the light switch and the tree flooded into colour. He opened the curtains and the light streamed out into the darkness. Almost every house in the valley was in darkness. Apart from a solitary light in the house next door they were alone. Either everyone had evacuated or they were all sleeping. Preparing for the danger which lay ahead.

Sleep. Bed.

It seemed a good idea. In theory.

Julie was standing beside him. She had her arms folded in front of her, instinctive defence. She was still in that dratted nightgown. Hadn't he asked her to take it off? Hadn't he warned her?

But she never had been a woman who followed orders, he thought. She'd always been self-contained, sure, confident of her place in the world. He'd fallen in love with that containment, with her fierce intelligence, with the humour that matched his, a biting wit that made him break into laughter at the most inappropriate moments. He'd loved her drive to be the best at her job. He'd understood and admired it because he was like that, too. It was only when the twins arrived that they'd realised two parents with driving ambition was a recipe for disaster.

Still they'd managed it. They'd juggled it. They'd loved...

Loved. He looked at her now, shivering despite the oppressive heat. She looked younger, he thought suddenly.

Vulnerable.

She'd never been vulnerable and neither had he.

But they'd loved.

'Julie?'

'Yes?' She looked at him and she looked scared. And he knew it was nothing to do with the fires.

'Mmm.'

'Let's go to bed,' he said, but she hugged her arms even tighter.

'I don't...know.'

'There's no one else?'

'No.'

'Nor for me,' he said gently. He was treading on eggshells here. He should back off, go and sleep in the spare room, but there was something about this woman… This woman who was still his wife.

'We can't…at least…I can't move forward,' he told her, struggling to think things through as he spoke. 'Relationships are for other people now, not for me. But tonight… For me, tonight is all about goodbye and I suspect it's goodbye for you as well.'

'The house won't burn.'

'No,' he said, even more gently. 'It probably won't. At dawn I'll go out and cut down the overhanging branches—and even with my limited skill with power tools, I should get them cleared before the wind changes. Then we'll turn on every piece of fire-safe technology we built into this house. And after that, no matter what the outcome, we'll walk away. We must. It's time it was over, Jules, but for tonight…' He hesitated but he had to say it. It was a gut-deep need and it couldn't be put aside. 'Tonight, we need each other.'

'So much for being strangers,' she whispered. She was still hugging herself, still contained. Sort of.

'I guess we are,' he conceded. 'I guess the people we've turned into don't know each other. But for now…for this night I'd like to take to bed the woman who's still my wife.'

'In name only.' She was shivering.

'So you don't want me? Not tonight? Never again?'

And she looked up at him with those eyes he remembered so well, but with every bit of the confidence, humour, wit and courage blasted right out of them.

'I *do* want you,' she whispered. 'That's what terrifies me.'

'Same here.'

'Rob…'

'Mmm.'

'Do you have condoms? I mean, the last thing…'

'I have condoms.'

'So when you said relationships are for other people…'

'Hey, I'm a guy.' He was trying again to make her smile. 'I live in hope. Hope that one morning I'll wake up and find the old hormones rushing back. Hope that one evening I'll look across a crowded room and see a woman laughing at the same dumb thing I'm laughing at.'

That had been what happened that night, the first time they'd met. It had been a boring evening: a company she worked for announcing a major interest in a new dockland precinct; a bright young architect on the fringes; Julie with her arms full of contracts ready to be signed by investors. A boring speech, a stupid pun missed by everyone, including the guy making the speech, and then eyes meeting...

Contracts handed to a junior. Excuses made fast. Dinner. Then...

'So I'm prepared,' Rob said gently and tilted her chin. Gently, though. Forcing her gaze to meet his. 'One last time, my Jules?'

'I'm not...your Jules.'

'Can you pretend...for tonight?'

And, amazingly, she nodded. 'I think... maybe,' she managed, and at last her arms uncrossed. At last she abandoned the defensive. 'Maybe because I need to drive the ghosts away. And maybe because I want to.'

'I need more than *maybe*, Jules,' he said gently. 'I need you to want me as much as I want you.'

And there was the heart of what she was up against. She wanted him.

She always had.

Once upon a time she'd stood before an altar, the perfect bride. She remembered walking down the aisle on her father's arm, seeing Rob waiting for her, knowing it was right. She'd felt like the luckiest woman in the world. He'd held her heart in his hand, and she'd known that he'd treat it with care and love and honour.

She'd said I do, and she'd meant it.

Until death do us part...

Death had parted them, she thought and it would go on keeping them apart. There was no way they could pick up the pieces that had been their lives before the boys.

But somehow they'd been given tonight.

One night. A weird window of space and time. Tomorrow the echoes of their past could well disappear, and maybe it was right that they should.

But tonight he was here.

Tonight he was gazing at her with a tenderness that told her he needed this night as well. He wanted that sliver of the past as much as she did.

For tonight he wanted her and she ached for him back. But he wasn't pushing. It had to be her decision.

Maybe I can do this, she thought. *Maybe, just for tonight, I can put my armour aside...*

Her everyday life was now orchestrated, rigidly contained. It held no room for emotional attachment. Even coming here was an aberration. Once the fire was over, she'd return to her job, return to her life, return to her containment.

But for now...that ache... The way Rob talked to her... That he asked her to his bed...

It was like a siren call, she thought helplessly.

She'd loved this man; she'd loved everything about him. Love had almost destroyed her and she couldn't go there again, but for tonight… Tonight was an anomaly—time out of frame.

For tonight, she was in her home with her husband. He wasn't pushing. He never had. He was simply waiting for her to make her decision.

Lie with her husband…or not?

Have one night as the Julie of old…or not?

'Because once we loved,' he said lightly, as if this wasn't a major leap, and maybe it wasn't. Maybe she could love again—just for the night. One night of Rob and then she'd get on with her life. One night…

'But not if you see it as scary.'

His gaze was locked on hers. 'It's for pleasure only, my Jules,' he said softly. 'No threats. No promises. No future. Just for this night. Just for us. Just for now. Maybe or yes? I need a yes, Jules. You have to be sure.'

And suddenly she was. 'Yes,' she said, because there was nothing else to say. 'Yes, please, Rob. For tonight, there's no maybe about it. Crazy or not, scary or not, I want you.'

'Hey, what's scary about me?' And he was laughing down at her, his lovely eyes dancing. Teasing. Just as he once had.

'That's just the problem,' she whispered. 'There's nothing crazy about the way I feel about you. *That's* what makes it so scary. But, scary or not, for tonight, Rob, for the last time, I want to be your wife.'

For those tense few minutes when they'd first seen each other, when they'd come together in the house for the first time in years, they'd made believe it was the first time. They were strangers. They'd relived that first connection.

Now…it was as if they'd pressed the fast forward on the replay button, Rob thought, and suddenly it was the first time he was to take her to bed.

But this was no make-believe, and it wasn't the first time. He knew everything there was to know about this woman. His wife.

But maybe that was wrong. Yes, he knew everything there was to know about the Julie of years ago, the Julie who'd married him, but there was a gaping hole of years. How had she filled it? He didn't know. He hardly knew how he'd filled it himself.

But for now, by mutual and unspoken consent, those four years didn't exist. Only the fierce magnetic attraction existed—the attraction that had him wanting her the moment he'd set eyes on her.

They hadn't ended up in bed on their first date, but it had nearly killed them not to. They'd lasted half an hour into their second date. He'd gone to her apartment to pick her up…they hadn't even reached the bedroom.

And now, here, the desire was the same. He'd seen her in her flimsy nightgown and he wanted her with every fibre of his being. And even if it was with caveats—*for the last time*—he tugged her into his arms and she melted.

Fused.

'You're sure?' he asked and she nodded and the sound she made was almost a purr. Memories had been set aside—the hurtful ones had, anyway.

'I'm sure,' she whispered and tugged his face close and her whisper was a breath on his mouth.

He lifted her and she curled against him. She looped her arms around his neck and twisted, so she could kiss him.

Somehow he made it to the bedroom door. The bed lay, invitingly, not ten feet away, but he had to stop and let himself be kissed. And kiss back.

Their mouths fused. It was like electricity, a fierce jolt on touching, then a force so great that neither could pull away. Neither could think of pulling away.

He had his wife in his arms. He couldn't think past that. He had his Julie and his mind blocked out everything else.

His wife. His love.

* * *

She'd forgotten how her body melted. She'd forgotten how her body merged into his. How the outside world disappeared. How every sense centred on him. Or on *them*, for that was how it was. Years ago, the moment he'd first touched her, she'd known what marriage was. She'd felt married the first time they'd kissed.

She'd abandoned herself to him then, as simple as that. She'd surrendered and he'd done the same. His lovely strong body, virile, heavy with the scent of aroused male, wanting her, taking her, demanding everything, but in such a way that she knew that if she pulled away he'd let her go.

Only she knew she'd never pull away. She couldn't and neither could he.

Their bodies were made for each other.

And now…now her mouth was plundering his, and his hers, and the sensations of years ago were flooding back. Oh, the taste of him. The feel… Her body was on fire with wanting, with the knowledge that somehow he was hers again, for however long…

Until morning?

No. She wasn't thinking that. It didn't matter how long. All that mattered was now.

Somehow, some way, they reached the bed, but even before they were on top of it she was fighting with the buttons of his shirt. She wanted this man's body. She wanted to feel the strength of him, the hardness of his ribs, the tightness of his chest. She wanted to taste the salt of him.

Oh, his body... It was hers; it still felt like hers.

Four years ago...

No. Forget four years. Just think about now.

His kiss deepened. Her nightgown was slipping away and suddenly it was easy. Memories were gone. All she could think of was him. All she wanted was him.

Oh, the feel of him. The taste of him.

Rob.

The years had gone. Everything had gone. There was only this man, this body, this moment.

'Welcome home, my love,' he whispered as their clothes disappeared, as skin met skin, as the night disappeared in a haze of heat and desire.

Home... There was so much unsaid in that word. It was a word of longing, a word of hope, a word of peace.

It meant nothing, she thought. It couldn't.

But her arms held him. Her mouth held him. Her whole body held him.

For this moment he was hers.

For this moment he was right. She was home.

* * *

He'd forgotten a woman could feel this good.

He'd forgotten…Julie?

But of course he hadn't. He'd simply put her in a place in his mind that was inaccessible. But now she was here, his, welcoming him, loving him.

She tasted fabulous. She still smelled like… like… He didn't know what she smelled like.

Had he ever asked her what perfume she wore? Maybe it was only soap. Fresh, citrus, it was in her hair.

He'd forgotten how erotic it was, to lie with his face in her tumbled hair, to feel the wisps around his face, to finger and twist and feel her body shudder as she responded to his touch.

The room was in darkness and that was good. If he could see her…her eyes might get that dead look, the look that said there was nothing left, for her or for him.

It was a look that had almost killed him.

But he wouldn't think of that. He couldn't, for her fingers were curved around his thighs, tugging him closer, closer…

His wife. His Julie. His own.

They loved and loved again. They melted into each other as if they'd never parted.

They loved.

He loved.

She was *his*.

The possessive word resonated in his mind, primeval as time itself. She was crying. He felt her tears, slipping from her face to his shoulder.

He gathered her to him and held, simply held, and he thought that at this moment if any man tried to take her his response would be primitive.

His.

Tomorrow he'd walk away. He'd accepted by now that their marriage was over, that Julie could never emerge from the thick armour she'd shielded herself with. In order to survive he needed to move on. He knew it. His shrink had said it. He knew it for the truth.

So he would walk away. But first…here was a gift he'd long stopped hoping for. Here was a crack in that appalling armour. For tonight she'd shed it.

'For tonight I'm loving you,' he whispered and she kissed him, fiercely, possessively, as if those vows they'd made so long ago still held.

And they did hold—for tonight—and that was all he was focusing on. There was no tomorrow. There was nothing but now.

He kissed her back. He loved her back.

'For tonight I'm loving you, too,' she whispered and she held him closer, and there was nothing in the world but his wife.

CHAPTER THREE

NOTE: IF A bush fire's heading your way, maybe you should set the alarm.

He woke and filtered sunlight was streaming through the cast windows. Filtered? That'd be smoke. It registered but only just, for Julie was in his arms, spooned against his body, naked, beautiful and sated with loving. It was hard to get his mind past that.

Past her.

But the world was edging in. The wind had risen. He could hear the sound of the gums outside creaking under the weight of it.

Wind. Smoke. Morning.

'Jules?'

'Mmm.' She stirred, stretched like a kitten and the sensation of her naked skin against his had him wanting her all over again. He could…

He couldn't. Wind. Smoke. Morning.

Somehow he hauled his watch from under his woman.

Eight-thirty.

Eight-thirty!

Get out by nine at the latest, the authorities had warned. Keep listening to emergency radio in case of updates.

Eight-thirty.

Somehow he managed to roll away and flick on the bedside radio. But even now, even realising what was at stake, he didn't want to leave her.

The radio sounded into life. Nothing had changed in this house. He'd paid to have a housekeeper come in weekly. The clock was still set to the right time.

There was a book beside the radio. He'd been halfway through it when…when…

Maybe this house should burn, he thought, memories surging back. Maybe he wanted it to.

'We should sell this house.' She still sounded sleepy. The implication of sleeping in hadn't sunk in yet, he thought, flicking through the channels to find the one devoted to emergency transmissions.

'So why did you come back?' he asked, abandoning the radio and turning back to her. The fire was important, but somehow…somehow he knew that words might be said now that could be said at no other time. Certainly not four years ago. Maybe not in the future either, when this house was sold or burned.

Maybe now…

'The teddies,' she told him, still sleepy. 'The wall-hanging my mum made. I…wanted them.'

'I was thinking of the fire engines.'

'That's appropriate.' Amazingly, she was smiling.

He'd never thought he'd see this woman smile again.

And then he thought of those last words. The words that had hung between them for years.

'Julie, it wasn't our fault,' he said and he watched her smile die.

'I…'

'I know. You said *you* killed them, but I believed it was me. That day I brought you home from hospital. You stood here and you said it was because you were sleeping and I said no, it wasn't anyone's fault, but there was such a big part of me that was blaming myself that I couldn't go any further. It was like…I was dead. I couldn't even speak. I've thought about it for four years. I've tried to write it down.'

'I got your letters.'

'You didn't reply.'

'I thought…the sooner you stopped writing the sooner you'd forget me. Get on with your life.'

'You know the road collapsed,' he said. 'You know the lawyers told us we could sue. You know it was the storm the week before that eroded the bitumen.'

'But that I was asleep...'

'We should have stayed in the city that night. We shouldn't have tried to bring the boys home. That's the source of our greatest regret, but it shouldn't be guilt. It put us in the wrong place at the wrong time. I've been back to the site. It was a blind curve. I rounded it and the road just wasn't there.'

'If we'd come up in broad daylight, when we were both alert...'

How often had he thought about this? How often had he screamed it to himself in the middle of troubled sleep?

He had to say it. He had to believe it.

'Jules, I manoeuvred a blind bend first. A tight curve. I wasn't speeding. I hit the brakes the moment I rounded the bend but the road was gone. If you'd been awake it wouldn't have made one whit of difference. Julie, it's not only me who's saying this. It was the police, the paramedics, the guys from the accident assessment scene.'

'But I can't remember.' It was a wail, and he tugged her back into his arms and thought it nearly killed him.

He was reassuring her but regardless of reason, the guilt was still there. *What if...? What if, what if, what if?*

Guilt had killed them both. Was killing them still.

He held her but her body had stiffened. The events of four years ago were right there. One night of passion couldn't wash them away.

He couldn't fix it. How could it be fixed, when two small beds lay empty in the room next door?

He kissed her on the lips, searching for an echo of the night before. She kissed him back but he could feel that she'd withdrawn.

Same dead Julie...

He turned again and went back to searching the radio channels. Finally he found the station he was looking for—the emergency channel.

'*...evacuation orders are in place now for Rowbethon, Carnarvon, Dewey's Creek... Leave now. Forecast is for forty-six degrees, with winds up to seventy kilometres an hour, gusting to over a hundred. The fire fronts are merging...*'

And all his attention was suddenly on the fire. It had to be. Rowbethon, Carnarvon, Dewey's Creek... They were all south of Mount Bundoon.

The wind was coming from the north.

'*Fire is expected to impact on the Mount Bun-*

doon area within the hour,' the voice went on. *'Bundoon Creek Bridge is closed. Anyone not evacuated, do not attempt it now. Repeat, do not attempt to evacuate. Roads are cut to the south. Fire is already impacting to the east. Implement your fire plans but, repeat, evacuation is no longer an option.'*

'We need to get to a refuge centre.' Julie was sitting bolt upright, wide-eyed with horror.

'There isn't one this side of the creek.' He glanced out of the window. 'We're not driving in this smoke. Besides, we have the bunker.' Thank God, they had the bunker.

'But…'

'We can do this, Jules.'

And she settled, just like that. Same old Jules. In a crisis, there was no one he'd rather have by his side.

'The fire plan,' she said. 'I have it.'

Of course she did. Julie was one of the most controlled people he knew. Efficient. Organised. A list-maker extraordinaire.

The moment they'd moved into this place she'd downloaded a Fire Authority Emergency Plan and made him go through it, step by step, making dot-points for every eventuality.

They were better off than most. Bush fire was always a risk in Australian summers and he'd thought about it carefully when he'd designed this place. The house had been built to withstand a furnace—though not an inferno. There'd been fires in Australia where even the most fireproof buildings had burned. But he'd designed the house with every precaution. The house was made of stone, with no garden close to the house. They had solar power, backup generators, underground water tanks, pumps and sprinkler systems. The tool shed doubled as a bunker and could be cleared in minutes, double-doored and built into earth. But still there was risk. He imagined everyone else in the gully would be well away by now and for good reason. Safe house or not, they were crazy to still be here.

But Julie wasn't remonstrating. She was simply moving on.

'I'll close the shutters and tape the windows while you clear the yard,' she said. Taping the windows was important. Heat could blast them inwards. Tape gave them an extra degree of strength and they wouldn't shatter if they broke.

'Wool clothes first, though,' she said, hauling a pile out of her bottom bedroom drawer, along with torches, wool caps and water bottles. Also a small fire extinguisher. The drawer had been set up years ago for the contingency of waking to fire. Efficiency plus.

Was it possible to still love a woman for her plan-making?

'I hope these extinguishers haven't perished,' she said, pulling a wool cap on her head and shoving her hair up into it. It was made of thick wool, way too big. 'Ugh. What do you think?'

'Cute.'

'Oi, we're not thinking cute.' But her eyes smiled at him.

'Hard not to. Woolly caps have always been a turn-on.'

'And I love a man in flannels.' She tossed him a shirt. 'You've been working out.'

'You noticed?'

'I noticed all night.' She even managed a grin. 'But it's time to stop noticing. Cover that six-pack, boy.'

'Yes, ma'am.' But he'd fielded the shirt while he was checking the fire map app on his phone, and what he saw made any thought of smiling back impossible.

She saw his face, grabbed the phone and her eyes widened. 'Rob...' And, for the first time, he saw fear. 'Oh, my...Rob, it's all around us. With this wind...'

'We can do this,' he said. 'We have the bunker.' His hands gripped her shoulders. Steadied her. 'Julie, you came up here for the teddies and the wall-hanging. Anything else?'

'Their...clothes. At least...at least some. And...'

She faltered, but he knew what she wanted to say. Their smell. Their presence. The last place they'd been.

He might not be able to save that for her, but he'd sure as hell try.

'And their fire engines,' he added, reverting, with difficulty, to the practical. 'Let's make that priority one. Hopefully, the pits are still clear.'

The pits were a fallback position, as well as the bunker. They'd built this house with love, but with clear acceptance that the Australian bush was designed to burn. Many native trees didn't regenerate without fire to crack their seeds. Fire was natural, and over generations even inevitable, so if you lived in the bush you hoped for the best and prepared for the worst. Accordingly, they'd built with care, insured the house to the hilt and didn't keep precious things here.

Except the memories of their boys. How did you keep something like that safe? How did you keep memories in fire pits?

They'd do their best. The pits were a series of holes behind the house, fenced off but easily accessed. Dirt dug from them was still heaped beside them, a method used by those who'd lived in the bush for generations. If you wanted to keep something safe, you buried it: put belongings inside watertight cases; put the cases in the pit; piled the dirt on top.

'Get that shirt on,' Julie growled, moving on with the efficiency she'd been born with. She cast a long regretful look at Rob's six-pack and then sighed and hauled on her sensible pants. 'Moving on… We knew we'd have to, Rob, and now's the time. Clearing the yard's the biggie. Let's go.'

The moment they walked out of the house they knew they were in desperate trouble. The heat took their breath away. It hurt to breathe.

The wind was frightening. It was full of dry leaf litter, blasting against their faces—a portent of things to come. If these leaves were filled with fire… She felt fear deep in her gut. The maps she'd just seen were explicit. This place was going to burn.

She wanted to bury her face in Rob's shoulder and block this out. She wanted to forget, like last night, amazingly, had let her forget.

But last night was last night. Over.

Concentrate on the list. On her dot-points.

'Windows, pits, shovel, go,' Rob said and seized her firmly by the shoulders and kissed her, hard and fast. Making a mockery of her determination that last night was over. 'We can do this, Jules. You've put a lot of work into that fire plan. It'd be a shame if we didn't make it work.'

They could, she thought as she headed for the shutters. They could make the fire plan work.

And maybe, after last night… Maybe…

Too soon. Think of it later. Fire first.

She fixed the windows—fast—then checked the pits. They were overgrown but the mounds of dirt were still loose enough for her to shovel. She could bury things with ease.

She headed inside, grabbed a couple of cases and headed into the boys' room.

And she lost her breath all over again.

She'd figured yesterday that Rob must have hired someone to clean this place on a regular basis. If it had been left solely to her, this house would be a dusty mess. She'd walked away and actively tried to forget.

But now, standing at their bedroom door, it was as if she'd just walked in for the first time. Rob would be carrying the boys behind her. Jiggling them, making them laugh.

Two and a half years old. Blond and blue-eyed scamps. Miniature versions of Rob himself.

They'd been sound asleep when the road gave way, then killed in an instant, the back of the car crushed as it rolled to the bottom of a gully.

The doctors had told her death would have been instant.

But they were right here. She could just tug back the bedding and Rob would carry them in.

Or not.

'Aiden,' she murmured. 'Christopher.'

Grief was all around her, an aching, searing loss. She hadn't let herself feel this for years. She hadn't dared to. It was hidden so far inside her she thought she'd grown armour that could surely protect her.

But the armour was nothing. It was dust, blown away at the sight of one neat bedroom.

It shouldn't be neat. It nearly killed her that it was neat. She wanted those beds to be rumpled. She wanted…

She couldn't want.

She should be thinking about fire, she thought desperately. The warnings were that it'd be on them in less than an hour. She had to move.

She couldn't.

The wind blasted on the windowpanes. She needed to tape them. She needed to bury memories.

Aiden. Christopher.

What had she been thinking, wondering if she could move on? What had she been doing, exposing herself to Rob again? Imagining she could still love.

She couldn't. Peeling back the armour, even a tiny part, allowed in a hurt so great she couldn't bear it.

'Julie?' It was a yell from just outside the window.

She couldn't answer.

'Julie!' Rob's second yell pierced her grief, loud and demanding her attention. 'Jules! If you're standing in that bedroom thinking of black you might want to look outside instead.'

How had he known what she was doing? Because he felt the same?

Still she didn't move.

'Look!' he yelled, even more insistent, and she had to look. She had to move across to the window and pull back the curtains.

She could just see Rob through the smoke haze. He was standing under a ladder, not ten feet from her. He had the ladder propped against the house.

He was carrying a chainsaw.

As she watched in horror he pulled the cord and it roared into life.

'What's an overhanging branch between friends?' he yelled across the roar and she thought: *He'll be killed. He'll be...*

'Mine's the easier job,' he yelled as he took his first step up the ladder. 'But if I can do this, you can shove a teddy into a suitcase. Put the past behind you, Julie. Fire. Now. Go.'

He was climbing a ladder with a chainsaw. Rob and power tools...

He was an architect, not a builder.

She thought suddenly of Rob, just after she'd agreed to marry him. He'd brought her to the mountains and shown her this block, for sale at a price they could afford.

'This can be our retreat,' he'd told her. 'Commute when we can, have an apartment in the city for when we can't.' And then he'd produced his trump card. A tool belt. Gleaming leather, full of bright shiny tools, it was a he-man's tool belt waiting for a he-man. He'd strapped it on and flexed his muscles. 'What do you think?'

'You're never thinking of building yourself?' she'd gasped and he'd grinned and held up a vicious-looking...she didn't have a clue what.

'I might need help,' he admitted. 'These things look scary. I was sort of thinking of a registered builder, with maybe a team of registered builder's assistants on the side. But I could help.'

And he'd grinned at her and she'd known there was nothing she could refuse this man.

Man with tool belt.

Man with ladder and chainsaw.

And it hit her then, with a clarity that was almost frightening. Yesterday when she'd woken up it had been just like the day before and the day before that. She'd got up, she'd functioned for the day, she'd gone to bed. She'd survived.

Life went on around her, but she didn't care.

Yesterday, when she'd told her secretary she was heading up to the Blue Mountains, Maddie had been appalled. 'It's dangerous. They're saying evacuate. Don't go there.'

The thing was, though, for Julie danger no longer existed. The worst thing possible had already happened. There was nothing else to fear.

But now, standing at the window, staring at Rob and his chainsaw, she realised that, like it or not, she still cared. She could still be frightened for someone. For Rob.

But fear hurt. Caring hurt. She didn't want to care. She couldn't. Somehow she had to rebuild the armour. But meanwhile...

Meanwhile Rob was right. She had to move. She had to bury teddies.

He managed to get the branches clear and drag them into the gully, well away from the house.

He raked the loose leaves away from the house, too, easier said than done when the wind was blasting them back. He blocked the gutters and set up the generator so they could use the pump and access the water in the tanks even if they lost the solar power.

He worked his way round the house, checking, rechecking and he almost ran into Julie round the other side.

The smoke was building. It was harder and harder to see. Even with a mask it hurt to breathe.

The heat was intense and the wind was frightening.

How far away was the fire? There was no way to tell. The fire map on his phone was of little use. It showed broad districts. What he wanted was a map of what was happening down the road. He couldn't see by looking. It was starting to be hard to see as far as the end of his arm.

'We've done enough.' Julie's voice was hoarse from the smoke. 'I've done inside and cleared the back porch. I've filled the pits and cleared the bunker. All the dot-points on the plan are complete.'

'Really?' It was weird to feel inordinately pleased that she'd remembered dot-points. Julie and her dot-points...weird that they turned him on.

'So what now?' she asked. 'Oh, Rob, I can't bear it in these clothes. All I want is to take them off and lie under the hose.'

It gave him pause for thought. *Jules, naked under water...* 'Is that included on our dots?' Impossible not to sound hopeful.

'Um…no,' she said, and he heard rather than saw her smile.

'Pity.'

'We could go inside and sit under the air-conditioning while it's still safe to have the air vents open.'

'You go in.' He wouldn't. How to tell what was happening outside if he was inside? 'But, Jules, the vents stay closed. We don't know where the fire is.'

'How can we tell where it is? How close…?' The smile had gone from her voice.

'It's not threatening. Not yet. We have thick smoke and wind and leaf litter but I can reach out my hand and still—sort of—see my fingers. The fire maps tell us the fire's cut the access road, but how long it takes to reach this gully is anyone's guess. It might fly over the top of us. It might miss us completely.' There was a hope.

'So…why not air-conditioning?'

'There's still fire. You can taste it and you can smell it. Even if the house isn't in the firing line, there'll be burning leaf litter swirling in the updraught. On Black Saturday they reckoned there were ember attacks five miles from the fire front. We'd look stupid if embers were sucked in through the vents. But you go in. I'll keep checking.'

'For…how long?' she faltered. 'I mean…'

'For as long as it takes.' He glanced upward, hearing the wind blasting the treetops, but there was no way he could see that far. The smoke was making his throat hurt, but still he felt the need to try and make her smile. 'It looks like we're stuck here for Christmas,' he managed. 'But I'm sure Santa will find a way through. What's his motto? *Neither snow nor rain nor heat nor gloom of night shall stay St Nicholas from the swift completion of his appointed rounds.*'

'Isn't that postmen?' And amazingly he heard the smile again and was inordinately pleased.

'Maybe it is,' he said, picking up his hose and checking pressure. They still had the solar power but he'd already swapped to the generators. There wouldn't be time to do it when… if…the fire hit. 'But I reckon we're all in the same union. Postmen, Santa and us. We'll work through whatever's thrown at us.' And then he set down his hose.

'It's okay, Jules,' he said, taking her shoulders. 'We've been through worse than this. We both know…that things aren't worth crying over. But our lives are worth something and maybe this house is worth something as well. It used to be a home. I know the teddies and fire engines and wall-hanging are safe but let's see this as a challenge. Let's see if we can save…what's left of the rest of us.'

* * *

They sat on the veranda and faced the wind. It was the dumbest place to sit, Julie thought, but it was also sensible. The wind seared their faces, the heat parched their throats but ember attacks would come from the north.

Their phones had stopped working. 'That'll be the transmission tower on Mount Woorndoo,' Rob said matter-of-factly, like it didn't matter that a tower not ten miles away had been put out of action.

He brought the battery radio outside and they listened. All they could figure was that the valley was cut off. All they could work out was that the authorities were no longer in control. There were so many fronts to this fire that no one could keep track.

Most bush fires could be fought. Choppers dropped vast loads of water, fire trucks came in behind the swathes the choppers cleared; communities could be saved.

Here, though, there were so many communities…

'It's like we're the last people in the world,' Julie whispered.

'Yeah. Pretty silly to be here.'

'I wanted to be here.'

'Me, too,' he said and he took her hand and held.

And somehow it felt okay. Scary but right.

They sat on. Surely the fire must arrive soon. The waiting was almost killing her, and yet, in a strange way, she felt almost calm. Maybe she even would have stayed if Rob hadn't come, she thought. Maybe this was...

'We're going to get through this,' Rob said grimly and she hauled her thoughts back from where they'd been taking her.

'You know, those weeks after the boys were killed, they were the worst weeks of my life.' He said it almost conversationally, and she thought: *don't. Don't go there*. They hadn't talked about it. They couldn't.

But he wasn't stopping. She should get up, go inside, move away, but he was waiting for ember attacks, determined to fight this fire, and she couldn't walk away.

Even if he was intent on talking about what she didn't want to hear.

'You were so close to death yourself,' he said, almost as if this had been chatted about before. 'You had smashed ribs, a punctured lung, a shattered pelvis. But that bang on the head... For the first few days they couldn't tell me how you'd wake up. For the first twenty-four hours they didn't even know whether you'd wake up at all. And there I was, almost scot-free. I had a laceration on my arm and nothing more. There were people everywhere—my parents, your parents, our friends. I was surrounded yet I'd never felt so alone. And at the funeral...'

'Don't.' She put a hand on his arm to stop him but he didn't stop. But maybe she had to hear this, she thought numbly. Maybe he had to say it.

'I had to bury them alone,' he said. 'Okay, not alone in the physical sense. The church was packed. My parents were holding me up but you weren't there... It nearly killed me. And then, when you got out of hospital and I asked if you'd go to the cemetery...'

'I couldn't.' She remembered how she'd felt. Where were her boys? To go to the cemetery... to see two tiny graves...

She'd blocked it out. It wasn't real. If she didn't see the graves, then maybe the nightmare would be just that. An endless dream.

'It was like our family ended right there,' Rob said, staring sightlessly out into the smoke. 'It didn't end when our boys died. It ended...when we couldn't face their death together.'

'Rob...'

'I don't know why I'm saying this now,' he said, almost savagely. 'But hell, Julie, I'm fighting this. Our family doesn't exist any more. I can't get back...any of it. But once upon a time we loved each other and that still means something. So if you're sitting here thinking it doesn't matter much if you go up in flames, then think again. Because, even though I'm not part of your life any more, if I lose you completely, then what's left of my sanity goes, too. So prepare to be protected, Jules. No fire is going to get what's left of what I once loved. Of what I still love. So I'm heading off to do a fast survey of the boundary, looking for embers. It'd be good if you checked closer to the house but you don't need to. I'll do it for both of us. This fire…I'll fight it with everything I have. Enough of our past has been destroyed. This is my line in the sand.'

CHAPTER FOUR

THE SOUND CAME before the fire. Before the embers. Before hell.

It was a thousand freight trains roaring across the mountains, and it was so sudden that they were working separately when it hit. It was a sweeping updraught which felt as if it was sucking all the air from her lungs. It was a mass of burning embers, not small spot fires they could cope with but a mass of burning rain.

Stand and fight... They knew as the rumble built to a roar that no man alive could stay and fight this onslaught.

Julie was fighting to get a last gush of water onto the veranda. A branch had blasted in against the wall and Rob had been dragging it away from the building. She couldn't see him.

He was somewhere out in the smoke, heading back to her. Please, she pleaded. Please let him be heading back to her.

She had the drill in her head. *When the fire*

hits, take cover in your designated refuge and wait for the front to pass. As soon as the worst has passed, you can emerge to fight for your home, but don't try and fight as the front hits. Take cover.

Now.

'Rob…' Where was he? She was screaming for him but she couldn't even hear herself above the roar. The heat was blasting in front of the fire, taking the temperature to unbearable levels. She'd have to head for the shelter without him…

Unthinkable!

But suddenly he was with her. Grabbing her, hauling her off the veranda. But, instead of heading towards the bunker, he was hauling her forward, into the heat. 'Jules, help me.'

'Help?' They had to get to the bunker. What else could they do?

'Jules, there are people next door.' He was yelling into her ear. 'There's a woman—pregnant, a mum. She was trying to back her car out of the driveway and she's hit a post. Jules, she won't come with me. We need to make her see sense. Forcibly if need be, and I can't do it by myself.'

And, like it or not, sensible or not, he had her arm. He was hauling her with him, stumbling across their yard, a yard which seemed so unfamiliar now that it was terrifying.

There were burning embers, burning leaves hitting her face. They shouldn't be here. They had to seek refuge. But…

'She's lost…a kid…' Rob was struggling to get enough breath to yell over the roar of impending fire. 'When the car hit, the dog got out. The kid's four years old, chasing his dog and she can't find him. I have to…' But then a blast of heat hit them, so intense he couldn't keep yelling. He just held onto her and ran.

But she wanted to be safe. She wanted this to be over. Why was Rob dragging her away from the bunker?

A child… Four years old? She tried to take it in but her mind wouldn't go there.

And then they were past the boundary post, not even visible now, only recognised because she brushed it as they passed. Then onto the gravel of the next-door neighbour's house. There was a car in the driveway, visible only as they almost ran into it.

She didn't know the neighbours. This house had been owned by an elderly couple when they'd built theirs. The woman had since died, her husband had left to live with his daughter and the house had stood empty and neglected for almost the entire time they'd lived here.

Last night she'd been surprised to see the lights. She and Rob had both registered that there'd been someone there, but then they'd both been so caught up...

And then her thoughts stopped. Through the wall of smoke, there was a woman. Slight. Shorter than she was.

Very, very pregnant.

Rob reached to grab her and held.

'I can't find him.' The woman was screaming. 'Help me! Help me!' The scream pierced even the roar of the fire and it held all the agony in the world. It was a wail of loss and desperation and horror.

'We will.' Rob grabbed Julie's arm, thrust the woman's hand into hers and clamped his own hand on top. 'Julie, don't let go and that's an order. Consider it a dot-point, the biggest one there is. Julie, Amina; Amina, Julie. Amina, Julie's taking you to safety. You need to go with her now. Julie, go.'

'But Danny...' The woman was still screaming.

'I'll find him. Julie, the bunker...'

'But you have to come, too.' Julie was screaming as well. Already they were cutting things so close they mightn't make it. The blackness was now tinged with burning orange, flashes looming out of the blasting heat. Dear God, they had to go—but they had to go together.

But Rob was backing away, yelling back at

her over the roar of the fire. 'Jules, there's a little boy.' His voice held a desperation that matched hers. 'He ran to find his dog. I won't let this one die. I won't. Go!'

And his words stopped her screaming. They stopped her even wanting to scream.

She checked for a moment, fought for air, fought for sanity. A wave of wind and heat smashed into her, almost knocking her from her feet. Burning embers were smashing against their clothes.

The woman was wearing a bulky black dress but it didn't hide her late pregnancy. Another child. Dear God…

And they didn't have to wait until the fire front hit them; the fire was here now.

'Jules, go!' Rob was yelling, pushing.

But still… 'I can't…leave you.'

'Danny…' The woman's scream was beyond terror, beyond reason, almost drowning Julie's, but Rob had heard her.

'Jules.' He touched her once, briefly, a hand on her cheek. A touch of reassurance where there was no reassurance to be had. A touch for courage. Then he pushed her again.

'Keep her and her little one safe. You can do this,' he said fiercely. 'But stay safe. I won't lose…more. I'll find him,' he said fiercely. 'Go!'

* * *

The woman had to be almost dragged to the bunker. Somewhere out there was her son, and Julie could feel her terror, could almost taste it, and it was nearly enough to drown her own fear.

Left on her own she'd be with Rob, no question. Did it matter if she died? Not much. But she was gripping her neighbour's hand and the woman looked almost to term. Two lives depended on her and Rob had told her what he expected.

And she expected it of herself. That one touch and she knew what she was doing couldn't be questioned.

But by now it was almost impossible to move. She hardly knew where the bunker was. The world was a swirling blast of madness. Trees loomed from nowhere. She could see nothing. How could she be lost in her own front yard?

She couldn't. She wouldn't. She had the woman's hand in a grip of iron and she kept on going, tugging the woman behind her.

Finally she reached the side of the house. There was no vision left at all now. The last of the light had gone. The world was all heat and smoke and fear.

She touched the house and kept touching as she hauled the woman along behind her. The woman had ceased fighting, but she could feel her heaving sobs. There was nothing she could do about that, though. Her only thought was to get to the rear yard, then keep going without deviation and the bunker would be right there.

But Rob…

Don't think of Rob.

There was so much smoke. How could they breathe?

And then the bunker was right in front of her groping arm. She'd been here earlier, checked it was clear. She should have left the door open. Now it was all she could do to haul it wide. She had to let Amina go and she was fearful she'd run.

If it was her little boy out there she'd run.

Christopher. Aiden…

Don't think it. That was the way of madness.

But Amina had obviously made a choice. She was no longer pulling back. Her maternal instincts must be tearing her apart. Her son was in the fire but she had to keep her baby safe. She was trusting in Rob.

Do not think of Rob.

Somehow she managed to haul open the great iron door Rob had built as the entrance to the bunker. The bunker itself was dug into the side of the hill, with reinforced earth on the sides and floor and roof, with one thick door facing the elements and a thinner one inside.

She got the outer door open, shoving the woman inside, fighting to keep out embers.

She slammed it shut behind her and it felt as if she was condemning Rob to death.

Inside the inner door was designed to keep out heat. She couldn't shut that. No way. The outer door would have to buckle before she'd consider it. One sheet of iron between Rob and safety was more than she could bear; two was unthinkable.

The woman was sobbing, crumpling downward. There were lamps by the door. She flicked one on, took a deep, clean breath of air that hardly had any smoke in it and took stock.

She was safe here. They were safe.

She wasn't sure what was driving her, what was stopping her crumbling as well, but she knew what she had to do. The drill. Her dot-points. Rob would laugh at her, say she'd be efficient to the point where she organised her own funeral.

He loved her dot-points.

She allowed herself one tiny sob of fear, then swallowed it and knelt beside the woman, putting her arm around the woman's shoulders.

'We're safe,' she told her, fighting to keep her voice steady. 'You and your baby are safe. This place is fireproof. Rob's designed it so we have ventilation. We have air, water, even food if we need. We can stay here until it's all over.'

'D...Danny.'

'Rob is with Danny,' she said with a certainty she had to assume. But suddenly it wasn't assumed. Rob had to be with Danny and Rob had to be safe. Anything else was unthinkable.

'Rob will have him,' she whispered. 'My... my husband will keep him safe.'

'Danny! Luka!' Why was he yelling? Nothing could be heard above the roar of the fire. He could see nothing. To stay out here and search for a child in these conditions was like searching in hot, blasting sludge. A child would be swallowed, as he was being swallowed.

He'd asked for the dog's name. 'Luka,' Amina had told him through sobs. 'A great big golden retriever my husband bought to keep us safe. Danny loves him.'

So now he added Luka to his yelling. But where in this inferno...?

He stopped and made himself think. The boy had followed the dog. Where would the dog go?

Back to the house, surely. He'd escaped from the car. He'd be terrified. If Danny had managed to follow him...

The heat was burning. He'd shoved a wool cap over his head. Now he pulled it right down over his eyes. He couldn't see anyway and it stopped the pain as embers hit. He had his hands out, blundering his way to the front door.

At least Julie was safe. It was the one thing that kept him sane, but if there was another tragedy out of this day…

He knew, none better, how close to the edge of sanity Julie had been. He knew how tightly she held herself together. How controlled…

He hadn't been able to get past that control and in the end he'd had to respect it. He'd had to walk away, to preserve them both.

If he died now maybe Julie's control would grow even deeper. The barriers could become impenetrable—or maybe the barriers would crumble completely.

Either option was unthinkable.

Last night he'd seen a glimmer of what they'd once had. Only a glimmer; the barriers had been up again this morning. But he'd seen underneath. How vulnerable…

He could go to her now. Save himself.

And sit in the bunker while another child died?

He had his own armour, his own barriers, and they were vulnerable, too. Another child's death…

'Danny! Luka!' He was screaming, and his screams were mixing with the fire.

'Please…'

* * *

Please.

She said it over and over again. She'd found water bottles. She'd given one to Amina, and watched her slump against the back wall, her face expressionless.

Her face looked dead.

Her face would look like that too, Julie thought. Maybe it had looked like that for four years?

She slumped down on the floor beside her. Fought to make her mind work.

What was safety when others weren't safe? When Rob was out there?

'Do you think…?' Amina whispered.

'I can't think,' Julie told her. She took a long gulp of water and realised just how parched she'd been. How much worse for Rob…

'So…so what do we do?' Amina whispered.

'Wait for Rob.'

'Your husband.'

'Yes.' He still was, after all. It was a dead marriage but the legalities still held.

'My…my husband will be trying to reach us,' Amina whispered. 'He's a fly in, fly out miner. He was flying back in last night. He rang from the airport and told us not to move until he got here. I'm not very good in the car but in the end I couldn't wait. But then I crashed.'

'What's his name?' She was trying so hard to focus on anything but Rob.

'Henry,' Amina said. 'He'll come. I know he will. I...I need him.'

You need Rob, Julie thought, but she didn't say it.

And she didn't say how much her life depended on Rob pushing through that door.

Amina's house had caught fire. Dear God, he could see flames through the blackness. The heat was almost unbearable. No, make that past unbearable.

He had to go. He was doing nothing staying here. He was killing himself in a useless hunt.

But still... His hand had caught the veranda rail. He steadied. One last try...

He hauled himself onto the veranda and gave one last yell.

'Danny! Luka!'

And a great heavy body shoved itself at his legs, almost pushing him over.

Dog. He couldn't see him. He could only crouch and hold.

He searched for his collar and found...a hand. A kid, holding the dog.

'Danny!' There was nothing of him, a sliver of gasping fear. He couldn't see. He hauled him into his arms and hugged, steadying for a moment, taking as well as giving comfort. Taking strength.

God, the heat...

'Mama...' the little boy whimpered, burying his face in Rob's chest, not because he trusted him, but to stop the heat.

Rob was holding him with one arm, unbuttoning his wool flannel shirt with the other. Thank God the shirt was oversized. The kid was in shorts and sandals!

He buttoned up again, kid inside, and the kid didn't move. He was past moving, Rob thought. He could feel his chest heaving as he fought for breath. His own breathing hurt.

He had him. Them. The dog was hard at his side, not going anywhere.

He had to get to the bunker. It was way past a safe time for them to get there but there was nowhere else.

Julie would be at the bunker. If she'd made it.

And he had something to fight for. For Rob, the last four years had passed in a mist of grey. He'd tried to get on with his life, he'd built his career, he'd tried to enjoy life again but, in truth, every sense had seemed dulled. Yet now, when the world around him truly was grey and thick with smoke, every one of his senses was alert, intent, focused.

He would make it to the bunker. He would save this kid.

He would make it back to Julie.

Please...

'Hold on,' he managed to yell to the kid, though whether the little boy could hear him over the roar of the flames was impossible to tell. 'Hold your breath, Danny. We're going to run.'

Amina was crying, not sobbing, not hysterical, but tears were running unchecked down her face.

Julie was past crying. She was past feeling. If Rob was safe he'd be here by now. The creek at the bottom of the gully was dry. Even if it had been running it was overhung with dense bush. There was no safe place except here.

She was the last, she thought numbly. Her boys had gone. Now Rob, too?

Last night had been amazing. Last night it had felt as if she was waking up from a nightmare, as if slivers of light were finally breaking through the fog.

She hadn't deserved the light. She might have known...

'Your husband...' Amina managed, and she knew the woman was making a Herculean effort to talk. 'He's...great.'

'I…yeah.' What to say? There was nothing to say.

'How long have you been married?'

She had to think. Was she still married? Sort of. Sort of not.

'Seven years,' she managed.

'No kids?'

'I…no.'

'I'm sorry,' Amina whispered, and the dead feeling inside Julie turned into the hard, tight knot she knew so well. The knot that threatened to choke her. The knot that had ended her life.

'It's too late, isn't it?' Amina whispered. 'They would have been here by now. It's too…'

'I don't know…'

And then she stopped.

A bang. She was sure…

It was embers crashing against the door. Surely.

She should have closed the inner door. It was the last of her dot-points.

Another bang.

She was up, scrambling to reach the door. But then she paused, forcing herself to be logical. She was trying desperately to think and somehow she managed to make her mind see sense. To open the outer door mid-fire would suck every trace of oxygen from the bunker, even if the fire didn't blast right in. She couldn't do that to Amina.

Follow the dot-points. Follow the rules.

The banging must have been flying embers. It must. But if not…

She was already in the outer chamber, hauling the inner door closed behind her, closing herself off from the inner sanctuary. 'Stay!' she yelled at Amina and Amina had the sense to obey.

With the inner door closed it was pitch-dark, but she didn't need to see. She was at the outer door. She could feel the heat.

She hauled up the latch and tugged, then hauled.

The door swung wide with a vicious blast of heat and smoke.

And a body. A great solid body, holding something. Almost falling in.

A huge, furry creature lunging against her legs.

'Get it…get it sh—'

Rob. He was beyond speech. He was beyond anything. He crumpled to his knees, gasping for air.

She knew what he'd been trying to say. She had to get the door shut. She did it but afterwards she never knew how. It felt as if she herself was being sucked out. She fought with the door, fought with everything she had, and finally the great latch Rob had designed with such foresight fell into place.

But still…the smoke… There was no air. She couldn't breathe.

It took effort, will, concentration to find the latch on the inner door but somehow she did. She tugged and Amina was on the other side. As soon as the latch lifted she had it open.

'Danny…' It was a quavering sob.

'He's here,' Rob managed and then slumped sideways into the inner chamber, giving way to the all-consuming black.

Rob surfaced to water. Cool, wondrous water, washing his face. Someone was letting water run over him. There was water on his head. The wool cap was nowhere. There was just water.

He shifted a little and tasted it, and heard a sob of relief.

'Rob…'

'Julie.' The word didn't quite come out, though. His mouth felt thick and swollen. He heard a grunt that must have been him but he couldn't do better.

'Let me hold you while you drink.' And she had him. Her arm was supporting his shoulders, and magically there was a bottle of water at his lips. He drank, gloriously grateful for the water, even more grateful that it was Julie who had him. He could see her by the dim light of the torch lamp. Julie…

'The…the boy…' Maybe it came out, maybe it didn't, but she seemed to understand what he said.

'Danny's safe; not even burned. His mother has him. They're pouring water over Luka's pads. His pads look like your face. You both look scorched, but okay. It's okay, Rob.' Her voice broke. 'You'll live. We'll all live, thanks to you.'

CHAPTER FIVE

How LONG DID they stay in the shelter? Afterwards they tried to figure it out, but at the time they had no clue. Time simply stopped.

The roar from outside built to a crescendo, a sound where nothing could be said, nothing heard. Maybe they should have been terrified, but for Julie and for Amina too, they'd gone past terror. Terror was when the people they loved were outside, missing. Now they were all present and accounted for, and if hell itself broke loose, if their shelter disintegrated, somehow it didn't matter because they were there.

Rob was there.

He roused himself after a while and pushed himself back against the wall. Julie wasn't sure where the black soot ended and burns began. None of his clothes were burned. His eyes seemed swollen and bloodshot, but maybe hers did too. There were no mirrors here.

Amina was cuddling Danny, but she was also cuddling the dog.

The dog had almost cost her son his life, Julie thought wonderingly, but as Amina poured water over Luca's paws and his tail gave a feeble wag of thanks, she thought: *this dog is part of their family.*

No wonder Danny ran after him. He was loved.

Love...

It was a weird concept. Four years ago, love had died. It had shrivelled inside her, leaving her a dried out husk. She'd thought she could never feel pain again.

But when she'd thought she'd lost Rob... The pain was still with her. It was like she'd been under anaesthetic for years, and now the drug had worn off. Leaving her exposed...

The noise...

She was sitting beside the dirt wall, next to Rob.

His hand came out and took hers, and held. Taking comfort?

Her heart twisted, and the remembered pain came flooding back. Family...

She didn't have family. Her family was dead.

But Rob was holding her hand and she couldn't pull away.

She stirred at some stage, found cartons of

juice, packets of crackers and tinned tuna. The others didn't speak while she prepared a sort of lunch.

Danny was the first to eat, accepting her offering with pleasure.

'We didn't have breakfast,' he told her. 'Mama was too scared. She was trying to pack the car; trying to ring Papa. I wanted toast but Mama said when we got away from the fire.'

'We're away from the fire now,' she told him, glancing sideways at Rob. She wasn't sure if his throat was burned. She wasn't sure...of anything. But he cautiously sipped the juice and then tucked into the crackers like there was no tomorrow.

The food did them all good. It settled them. *Nothing like a good cup of tea*—Julie's Gran used to say that, and she grinned. There was no way she could attempt to boil water. Juice would have to do as a substitute, but it seemed to be working just as well.

The roaring had muted. She was scarcely daring to hope, but maybe the front had passed.

'It's still too loud and too hot,' Rob croaked. 'We can't open the door yet.'

'My Henry will be looking for us,' Amina said. 'He'll be frantic.'

'He won't have been allowed through,' Rob

told her. 'I came up last night and they were closing the road blocks then.'

'You were an idiot for coming,' Julie said.

'Yep.' But he didn't sound like he thought he
was an idiot. 'How long have you lived here?'
he asked Amina, and Julie thought he was trying hard to sound like things were normal. Like
this was just a brief couple of hours of enforced
stay and then they'd get on with their lives.

Maybe she would, she thought. After all, what
had changed for her? Maybe their house had
burned, but she didn't live here anyway.

Maybe more traces of their past were gone,
but they'd been doomed to vanish one day.
Things were just…things.

'Nearly four years,' Amina said. 'We came
just after Danny was born. But this place…it's
always been empty. The guy who mows the
lawns said there was a tragedy. Kids…' And
then her hand flew to her mouth. 'Your kids,'
she whispered in horror. 'You're the parents of
the twins who died.'

'It was a long time ago,' Rob said quietly. 'It's
been a very long time since we were parents.'

'But you're together?' She seemed almost
frantic, overwhelmed by past tragedy when re-
cent tragedy had just been avoided.

'For now we are,' Rob told her.

'But you don't live here.'

'Too many ghosts,' Julie said.

'Why don't you sell?' She seemed dazed beyond belief. Horror piled upon horror…

'Because of the ghosts,' Julie whispered.

Amina glanced from Julie to Rob and back again, her expression showing her sheer incomprehension of what they must have gone through. Or maybe it wasn't incomprehension. She'd been so close herself…

'If you hadn't saved Danny…' she whispered.

'We did,' Rob told her.

'But it can't bring your boys back.'

'No.' Rob's voice was harsh.

'There's nothing…' Amina was crying now, hugging Danny to her, looking from Julie to Rob and back again. 'You've saved us and there's nothing I can do to thank you. No way… I wish…'

'We all wish,' Rob said grimly, glancing at Julie. 'But at least today we have less to wish for. A bit of ointment and the odd bandage for Luka's sore paws and we'll be ready to carry on where we left off.'

Where we left off yesterday, though, Julie thought bleakly. *Not where we left off four years ago.*

What had she been about, clinging to this man last night? The ghosts were still all around them.

The ghosts would never let them go.

'We're okay,' Rob said and suddenly he'd tugged her to him and he was holding. Just holding. Taking comfort or giving it, it didn't matter. His body was black and filthy and big and hard and infinitely comforting and she had a huge urge to turn and kiss him, smoke and all. She didn't. She couldn't and it wasn't just that they were with Amina and Danny.

The ghosts still held the power to hold them apart.

An hour later, Rob finally decreed they might open the bunker doors. The sounds had died to little more than high wind, with the occasional crack of falling timber. The battery-operated radio Rob had dug up from beneath a pile of blankets told them the front had moved south. Messages were confused. There was chaos and destruction throughout the mountains. All roads were closed. The advice was not to move from where they were.

They had no intention of moving from where they were, but they might look outside.

The normal advice during a bush fire was to take shelter while the front passed, and then emerge as soon as possible and fight to keep the house from burning. That'd be okay in a fast-moving grass fire but down in the valley the bush had caught and burned with an intensity that was never going to blow through. There'd been an hour of heat so intense they could feel it through the double doors. Now…she thought they'd emerge to nothing.

'What about staying here while we do a reconnaissance?' Rob asked Amina and the woman gave a grim nod.

'Our house'll be gone anyway; I know that. What's there to see? Danny, can you pass me another drink? We'll stay here until Rob and Julie tell us it's safe.'

'I want to see the burned,' Danny said, and Julie thought this was becoming an adventure to the little boy. He had no idea how close he'd come.

'You'll see it soon enough.' Rob managed to keep the grimness from his voice. 'But, for now, Julie and I are the fearless forward scouts. You're the captain minding the fort. Take care of everyone here, Danny. You're in charge.'

And he held out his hand to Julie. 'Come on, love,' he said. 'Let's go face the music.'

She hesitated. There was so much behind those words. Sadness, tenderness, and…caring? How many years had they been apart and yet he could still call her *love*.

It twisted her heart. It made her feel vulnerable in a way she couldn't define.

'I'm coming,' she said, but she didn't take his hand. 'Let's go.'

First impression was black and smoke and heat. The wash of heat was so intense it took her breath away.

Second impression was desolation. The once glorious bushland that had surrounded their home was now a blackened, ash-filled landscape, still smouldering, flickers of flame still orange through the haze of smoke.

Third impression was that their house was still standing.

'My God,' Rob breathed. 'It's withstood… Julie, Plan D now.'

And she got it. Their fire plan had been formed years before but it was typed up and laminated, pasted to their bathroom door so they couldn't help but learn it.

Plan A: leave the area before the house was threatened. When they'd had the boys, this was the most sensible course of action. Maybe it was the most sensible course of action anyway. Their independent decision to come into a fire zone had been dumb. But okay, moving on.

Plan B: stay in the house and defend. They'd

abandon that plan if the threat was dire, the fire intense.

Plan C: head to the bunker and stay there until the front passed. And then implement Plan D.

Plan D: get out of the bunker as soon as possible and try to stop remnants of fire destroying the house.

The fire had been so intense that Julie had never dreamed she'd be faced with Plan D but now it had happened, and the list with its dot-points was so ingrained in her head that she moved into automatic action.

The generator was under the house. The pump was under there too. If they were safe they could pump water from the underground tanks.

'You do the water, spray the roof,' Rob snapped. 'I'll check inside, then head round the foundations and put out spot fires.' It was still impossibly hard to speak. Even breathing hurt, but somehow Rob managed it. 'We can do this, Julie. With this level of fire, we might be stuck here for hours, if not days. We need to keep the house safe.'

Why? There was a tiny part of her that demanded it. *Why bother?*

For the same reason she'd come back, she thought. This house had been home. It no longer was, or she'd thought it no longer was. But Rob was already heading for the bricked-in cavity under the house where they'd find tools to defend.

Rob thought this place was worth fighting for—the remnants of her home?

Who knew the truth of it? Who knew the logic? All she knew was that Rob thought this house was worth defending and, for now, all she could do was follow.

They worked solidly for two hours. After the initial checks they worked together, side by side. Rob's design genius had paid off. The house was intact but the smouldering fires after the front were insidious. A tiny spark in leaf litter hard by the house could be enough to turn the house into flames hours after the main fire. So Julie sprayed while Rob ran along the base of the house with a mop and bucket.

The underground water tank was a lifesaver. The water flowing out seemed unbelievably precious. Heaven knew how people managed without such tanks.

They didn't, she thought grimly as finally Rob left her to sentry duty and determinedly made his way through the ash and smoke to check Amina's house.

He came back looking even grimmer than he had when he'd left.

'Gone,' he said. 'And their car… God help

them if they'd stayed in that car, or even if they'd made it out onto the road. Our cars are still safe in the garage, but a tree's fallen over the track leading into the house. It's big and it's burning. We're going nowhere.'

There was no more to be said. They worked on. Maybe someone should go back to Amina to tell her about her house, but the highest priority had to be making sure this house was safe. Not because of emotional ties, though. This was all about current need.

Mount Bundoon was a tiny hamlet and this house and Amina's were two miles out of town. Thick bush lay between them and the township. There'd be more fallen logs—who knew what else—between them and civilisation.

'We'll be stuck here till Christmas,' Julie said as they worked, and her voice came out strained. Her throat was so sore from the smoke.

'Seeing as Christmas is tomorrow, yes, we will,' Rob told her. 'Did you have any plans?'

'I…no.'

'Do we have a turkey in the freezer?'

'I should have left it out,' she said unsteadily. 'It would have been roasted by now. Oh, Rob…' She heard her voice shake and Rob's arms came round her shoulders.

'No matter. We've done it. We're almost on the other side, Jules, love.'

But they weren't, she thought, and suddenly bleakness was all around her. What had changed? She could cling to Rob now but she knew that, long-term, they'd destroy each other. How could you help ease someone else's pain when you were withered inside by your own?

'Another half hour and we might be able to liberate Amina,' Rob said and something about the way he spoke told her he was feeling pretty much the same sensations she was feeling. 'The embers are getting less and Luka must be just about busting to find a tree by now.'

'Well, good luck to him finding one,' she said, pausing with her wet mop to stare bleakly round at the moonscape destruction.

'We can help them,' Rob said gently. 'They've lost their house. We can help them get through it. I don't know about you, Jules, but putting my head down and working's been the only thing between me and madness for the last four years. So keeping Amina's little family secure—that's something we can focus on. And we can focus on it together.'

'Just for the next twenty-four hours.'

'That's all I ever think about,' Rob told her, and the bleakness was back in his voice full force. 'One day at a time. One hour at a time. That's survival, Jules. We both know all about it so let's put it into action now.'

* * *

One day at a time? Rob worked on, the hard physical work almost a welcome relief from the emotions of the last twenty-four hours but, strangely, he'd stopped thinking of now. He was putting out embers on autopilot but the rest of his brain was moving forward.

Where did he go from here?

Before the fire, he'd thought he had almost reached the other side of a chasm of depression and self-blame. There'd been glimmers of light when he'd thought he could enjoy life again. 'You need to move on,' his shrink had advised him. 'You can't help Julie and together your grief will make you self-destruct.' Or maybe that wasn't what the shrink had advised him— maybe it was what the counselling sessions had made him accept for himself.

But now, working side by side, with Julie a constant presence as they beat out the spot fires still flaring up against the house, it was as if that thinking was revealed for what it was—a travesty. A lie. How could he move on? He still felt married. He still *was* married.

He'd fallen in love with his dot-point-maker, his Julie, eight years ago and that love was still there.

Maybe that was why he'd come back—drawn

here because his heart had never left the place. And it wasn't just the kids.

It was his wife.

So… Twenty-four hours on and the mists were starting to clear.

Together your grief will make you self-destruct. It might be true, he conceded, but Julie chose that moment to thump a spark with a wet mop. 'Take that, you—' she grunted and swiped it again for good measure and he found himself smiling.

She was still under there—his Julie.

Together they'd self-destruct? Maybe they would, he conceded as he worked, but was it possible—was there even a chance?—that together they could find a way to heal?

It was time to get Amina and Danny and Luka out of the bunker.

It was dark, not because it was night—it was still mid-afternoon—but because the smoke was still all-enveloping. They'd need to keep watch, take it in turns to check for spot fires, but, for now, they entered the house together.

Rob was holding Amina's hand. He'd been worried she'd trip over the mass of litter blasted across the yard. Danny was clinging to his mother's other side. Luka was pressing hard against his small master. The dog was limping a little but he wasn't about to leave the little boy.

Which left Julie bringing up the rear. She stood aside as Rob led them indoors and for some crazy reason she thought of the day Rob had brought her here to show her his plans. He'd laid out a tentative floor plan with string and markers on the soil. He'd shown her where the front door would be and then he'd swung her into his arms and lifted her across.

'Welcome to your home, my bride,' he'd told her and he'd set her down into the future hall and he'd kissed her with a passion that had left her breathless. 'Welcome to your Happy Ever After.'

Past history. Moving on. She followed them in and felt bleakness envelop her. The house was grey, dingy, appalling. There were no lights. She flicked the switch without hope and, of course, there was none.

'The cabling from the solar system must have melted,' Rob said, and then he gave a little-boy grin that was, in the circumstances, totally unexpected and totally endearing. 'But I have that covered. I knew the conduit was a weak spot when we built so the electrician's left me backup. I just need to unplug one lot and plug in another. The spare's in the garage, right next to my tool belt.'

And in the face of that grin it was impossible

not to smile back. The grey lifted, just a little. Man with tool belt, practically chest-thumping…

He'd designed this house to withstand fire. Skilled with a tool belt or not, he had saved them.

'It might take a bit of fiddling,' Rob conceded, trying—unsuccessfully—to sound modest. 'And the smoke will be messing with it now. But even if it fails completely we have the generator for important things, like pumping water. We have the barbecue. We can manage.'

'If you're thinking of getting up on the roof, Superman…'

'When it cools a little. And I'll let you hold the ladder.' He offered it like he was offering diamonds and, weirdly, she wanted to laugh. Her world was somehow righting.

'Do you mind…if we stay?' Amina faltered and Julie hauled herself together even more. Amina had lost her home. She didn't know where her husband was and Julie knew she was fearful that he'd have been on the road trying to reach her. What was Julie fearful about? Nothing. Rob was safe, and even that shouldn't matter.

But it did. She looked at his smoke-stained face, his bloodshot eyes, his grin that she knew was assumed—she knew this man and she knew he was feeling as bleak as she was, but he was trying his best to cheer them up—and she thought: *no matter what we've been through, we have been through it.*

I know this man. The feeling was solid, a rock in a shifting world. Even if being together hurt so much she couldn't bear it, he still felt part of her.

'Of course you can stay.' She struggled to sound normal, struggled to sound like a friendly neighbour welcoming a friend. 'For as long as you like.'

'For as long as we must,' Rob amended. 'Amina, the roads will be blocked. There's no phone reception. I checked and the transmission towers are down.' He hesitated and looked suddenly nervous. 'When...when's your baby due?'

'Not for another four weeks. Henry works in the mines, two weeks on, two weeks off, but he's done six weeks in a row so he can get a long leave for the baby. He was flying in last night. He'll be frantic. I have to get a message to him.'

'I don't think we can do that,' Rob told her. 'The phones are out and the road is cut by fallen timber. It's over an hour's walk at the best of times down to the highway and frankly it's not safe to try. Burned trees will still be falling. I don't think I can walk in this heat and smoke.'

'I wouldn't want you to, but Henry...'

'He'll have stopped at the road blocks. He'll

be forced to wait until the roads are cleared, but the worst of the fire's over. You'll see him soon.'

'But if the fire comes back…'

'It won't,' Rob told her. 'Even if there's a wind change, there's nothing left to burn.'

'But this house…'

'Is a fortress,' Julie told her. 'It's the house that Rob built. No fire dare challenge it.'

'He's amazing,' Amina managed as Rob headed out to do another mop and bucket round—they'd need to keep checking for hours, if not days. 'He's just…a hero.'

'He is.'

'You're so lucky…' And then Amina faltered, remembering. 'I mean… I can't…'

'I am lucky,' Julie told her. 'And yes, Rob's a hero.' And he was. Not her hero but a hero. 'But for now…for now, let's investigate the basics. We need to make this house liveable. It's Christmas tomorrow. Surely we can do something to celebrate.'

'But my Henry…'

'He'll come,' Julie said stoutly. 'And when he does, we need to have Christmas waiting for him.'

Rob made his way slowly round the house, inspecting everything. Every spark, every smouldering leaf or twig copped a mopful of water, but the threat was easing.

The smoke was easing a little. He could almost breathe.

He could almost think.

He'd saved Danny.

It should feel good and it did. He should feel lucky and he did. Strangely, though, he felt more than that. It was like a huge grey weight had been lifted from his shoulders.

Somehow he'd saved Danny. Danny would grow into a man because of what he'd achieved.

It didn't make the twins' death any easier to comprehend but somehow the knot of rage and desolation inside him had loosened a little.

Was it also because he'd held Julie last night? Lost himself in her body?

Julie.

'I wish she'd been able to save him, too,' he said out loud. Nothing and no one answered. It was like he was on Mars.

But Julie was here, right inside the door. And Amina and the kid he'd saved.

If he hadn't come, Julie might not have even made it to the bunker. Her eyes said maybe that wouldn't matter. Sometimes her eyes looked dead already.

How to fix that? How to break through?

He hadn't been able to four years ago. What was different now?

For the last four years he'd missed her with an ache in his gut that had never subsided. He'd learned to live with it. He'd even learned to have fun despite it, dating a couple of women this year, putting out tentative feelers, seeing if he could get back to some semblance of life. For his overtures to Julie had been met with blank rebuttal and there'd been nothing he could do to break through.

Had he tried hard enough? He hadn't, he conceded, because he'd known it was hopeless. He was part of her tragedy and she had to move on.

He'd accepted his marriage was over in everything but name.

So why had he come back here now? Was it really to save two fire engines? Or was it because he'd guessed Julie would be here?

One last hope...

If so, it had been subconscious, acting against the advice of his logic, his shrink, his new-found determination to look forward, to try and live.

But the thing was...Julie was here. She was here now, and it wasn't just the bleak, dead Julie. He could make this Julie smile again. He could reach her.

But every time he did, she closed off again.

No matter. She was still in there, in that house,

and he wielded his mop with extra vigour because of it. His Julie was still Julie. She was behind layers of protection so deep he'd need a battering ram to knock them down, but hey, he'd saved a kid and his house had withstood a firestorm.

All he needed now was a battering ram and hope.

And a miracle?

Miracles were possible. They'd had two today. Why not hope for another?

The house was hot, stuffy and filled with smoke but compared to outside it seemed almost normal. It even felt normal until she hauled back the thick shutters and saw outside.

The once glorious view of the bushland was now devastation.

'I don't know what to do,' Amina whimpered and Julie thought: *neither do I.* But at least they were safe; Rob was outside in the heat making sure of it. The option of whimpering, too, was out of the question.

She looked at Amina and remembered how she'd felt at the same stage in pregnancy. Amina wasn't carrying twins—at least she didn't think so—but this heat would be driving her to the edge, even without the added terrors of the fire.

'We have plenty of water in the underground

tank,' she told her. 'And we have a generator running the pumps. If you like, you could have a bath.'

'A bath…' Amina looked at Julie like she'd offered gold. 'Really?'

'Really.'

'I'm not sure I could get in and out.' She gazed down at her bulk and even managed a smile. 'I used to describe it as a basketball. Now I think it's a small hippopotamus.'

'There are safety rails to help you in and out.'

'You put them in when you were pregnant?' It was a shy request, not one that could be snapped at.

'Yes.'

'You and Rob didn't come back here because this is where your boys lived?' Amina ventured, but it wasn't really a question. It was a statement; a discovery.

'Yes.' There was no other answer.

'Maybe I'd have felt the same if I'd lost Danny.' Danny was clinging to her side but he was looking round, interested, oblivious to the danger he'd been in mere hours before. 'Danny, will you come into the bathroom with me?'

But Danny was looking longingly out of the window. He was obviously aching for his adventure to continue, and the last thing Amina needed, Julie thought, was her four-year-old in the bathroom with her.

Luka had flopped on the floor. The big dog gave a gentle whine.

'I'll see to his pads,' Amina said but she couldn't disguise her exhaustion, or her desolation at postponing the promised bath.

'Tell you what,' Julie said. 'You go take a bath and Danny and I will take Luka into the laundry. There's a big shallow shower/bath in there. If he's like any golden retriever I know he'll like water, right?'

'He loves it.'

'Then he can stand under the shower for as long as he wants until we know his pads are completely clean. Then I'll find some burn salve for them. Danny, will you help me?'

'Give Luka a shower?' Danny ventured.

'That's the idea. You can get undressed and have a shower with him if you want.' And Julie's mind, unbidden, was taking her back, knowing what her boys loved best in the world. 'We could have fun.'

Fun... Where had that word come from? Julie McDowell didn't do fun.

'Will Rob help, too?' Danny asked shyly and she nodded.

'When he's stopped firefighting, maybe he will.'

'Rob's big.' There was already a touch of hero worship in the little boy's voice.

'Yes.'

'He made me safe. I was frightened and he made me safe.'

'He's good at that,' Julie managed, but she didn't know where to take it from there.

Once upon a time Rob had made her feel safe. Once upon a time she'd believed safe was possible.

Right now, that was what he was doing. Keeping them safe.

One day at a time, she thought. She'd been doing this for years, taking one day at a time. But now Rob was outside, keeping them safe, and the thought left her exposed.

One day at a time? Right now she was having trouble focusing on one *moment* at a time.

Rob did one final round of the house and decided that was it; he didn't have the strength to stay in the heat any longer. But the wind had died, there was no fire within two hundred yards of the house and even that was piles of ash, simmering to nothing. He could take a break. He headed up the veranda steps and was met by the sound of a child's laughter.

It stopped him dead in his tracks.

He was filthy. He was exhausted. All he

wanted was to stand under a cold shower and then collapse, but the shower was in the laundry.

And someone was already splashing and shouting inside.

He could hear Julie laughing and, for some weird reason, the sound made him want to back away.

Coward, he told himself. He'd faced a bush fire and survived. How could laughter hurt so much? But it took a real effort to open the laundry door.

What met him was mess. Huge mess. The huge laundry shower-cum-bath had a base about a foot deep. It had been built to dump the twins in when they'd come in filthy from outside. The twins had filled it with their chaos and laughter and it was filled now.

More than filled.

Luka was sitting serenely in the middle of the base. The water was streaming over the big dog, and he had his head blissfully raised so the water could pour right over his eyes. Doggy heaven.

Danny had removed his clothes. He was using…one of the twins' boats?…to pour water over Luka's back. Every time he dumped a load, Luka turned and licked him, chin to forehead. Danny shrieked with laughter and scooped another load.

Julie was still fully dressed. She'd hauled off

her boots and flannel overshirt but the rest was intact. Dressed or not, though, she was sitting on the edge of the tub, her feet were in the water and she was soaking. Water was streaming over her hair. She was still black but the black was now running in streaks. She looked like she didn't care.

She was helping Danny scoop water. She was laughing with Danny, hugging Luka.

Silly as a tin of worms...

Once upon a time Rob's dad had said that to him. Angus McDowell, Rob's father, was a Very Serious Man, a minister of religion, harsh and unyielding. He'd disapproved of Julie at first, though when Julie's business prowess had been proven he'd unbent towards her. But he'd visited once and listened to Julie playing with the twins at bathtime.

'She's spoiling those two lads. Listen to them. Silly as a tin of worms.'

Right now her hair was wet, the waves curling, twisting and spiralling. He'd loved her hair.

He loved her hair.

How had he managed without this woman for so long?

The same way he'd managed without his boys, he told himself harshly. One moment at a time. One step after another. Getting through each day, one by one.

Julie must feel the same. He'd seen the death of the light behind her eyes. Being together, their one-step-at-a-time rule had faltered. They could only go on if they didn't think, didn't let themselves remember.

But Julie wasn't dead now. She was very much alive. Her eyes were dancing with pleasure and her laughter was almost that of the Julie of years ago. Young. Free.

She turned and saw him and the laughter faded, just like that.

'Rob!' Danny said with satisfaction. 'You're all black. Julie says she doesn't have enough soap to get all the black off.'

'There's enough left.' Julie rose quickly—a little too quickly. Before he could stop himself he'd reached out and caught her. He held her arms as she stepped over the edge of the bath. She was soaking. She'd been using some sort of lemon soap, the one she'd always used, and suddenly he realised where that citrus scent came from. She smelled... She felt...

'You're not clean yet,' he managed and she smiled. She was only six inches away from him. He was holding her. He could just tug...

He didn't tug. This was Julie. She'd been laughing and the sight of him had stopped that laughter.

They'd destroy each other. They'd pretty much

decided that, without ever speaking it out loud. Four years ago they'd walked away from each other for good reason.

How could you live with your own hurt when you saw it reflected in another's eyes, day after day? Moment after moment.

A miracle. He needed a miracle.

It's Christmas, he thought inconsequentially. *That's what I want for Christmas, Santa. I've saved Danny. We're safe and our house is safe, but I'm greedy. A third miracle. Please...*

'I'm clean apart from my clothes,' Julie managed, shaking her hair like a dog so that water sprayed over him. It hit his face, cool and delicious. Some hit his lips and he tasted it. Tasted Julie?

'I'll go change if you can take over here,' Julie said. 'Danny, is it okay if Rob comes under the water, too?'

'Yes,' Danny said. 'He's my friend. But you can both fit.'

'I need to find some clean clothes and something your mum can wear,' Julie told him. 'And some dog food. And some food for us.'

'The freezer...'

'I've hooked it to the generator so I can save the solar power for important stuff,' she said and deliberately she tugged away from him. It hurt that she pulled back. He wanted to hold her. 'Like the lights on the Christmas tree.'

'So we have Christmas lights and there's enough to eat?' he asked, trying hard to concentrate on practicalities.

'If need be, we have enough to live on for weeks.'

'Will we stay here for weeks?' Danny asked and Rob saw a shadow cross Julie's face. It was an act then, he thought, laughing and playing with the child. The pain was still there. She'd managed to push it away while she'd helped Danny have fun but it was with her still. Every time she saw a child…

And every time she saw him. She glanced up at him and he saw the hurt, the bleakness and the same certainty that this was a transient, enforced connection. If they were to survive they had to move on.

He knew it for the truth. It was time it lost the power to hurt.

Miracles were thin on the ground. They'd already had two today. Was it too much to ask for just one more?

How long was frozen food safe? Where was the Internet when she needed it? Finally she decided to play safe. Using the outside barbecue—well, it had been outside but Rob had hauled it under the house during the fire so now it could be wheeled outside again—she boiled dried spaghetti and tipped over a can of spaghetti sauce. The use-by dates on both were well past, but she couldn't figure how they could go off.

'I reckon, come Armageddon, these suckers will survive,' she told Rob, tipping in the sauce.

'We might have to do something a bit more imaginative tomorrow,' Rob told her. Washed and dressed in clean jeans and T-shirt, he'd found her in the kitchen. He was now examining the contents of the freezer. 'Shall I take the turkey out?'

'Surely the roads will be open by tomorrow.'

'Don't count on it,' he said grimly. 'Jules, I've been listening to the radio and the news is horrendous. We're surrounded by miles of burned ground and the fire's ongoing. The authorities won't have the resources to get us out while they're still trying to protect communities facing the fire front.'

'Turkey it is, then,' she said, trying to make it sound light. As if being trapped here was no big deal.

As if the presence of this man she'd once known so well wasn't doing things to her head. And to her body.

She'd known him so well. She *knew* him so well.

One part of her wanted to turn away from the barbecue right now and tug him into her arms. To hold and be held. To feel what she used to take for granted.

Another part of her wanted to leave right now, hike the miles down the road away from the mountains. Sure, it would entail risks but staying close to this man held risks as well. Like remembering how much she wanted him. Like remembering how much giving your heart cost.

It had cost her everything. There was simply…nothing left.

'Can…can I help?' Amina stood at the doorway, Danny clinging by her side. She was dressed in a borrowed house robe of Julie's. She looked lost, bereft, and very, very pregnant.

'Put your feet up inside,' Rob said roughly and Julie knew by his tone that he was as worried as she was about the girl. 'It's too hot out here already and Julie's cooking. Hot food!'

'You tell me where we can get sandwiches or salad and I'll open my purse,' Julie retorted. 'Sorry, Amina, it's spaghetti or nothing.'

'I'd like to see my house,' she said shyly and Julie winced.

'It's gone, Amina.'

'Burned,' Danny said. The adventure had gone out of the child. He looked scared.

'Yes, but we have this house,' Julie said.

'That's something. You can stay here for as long as you want.'

'My husband will be looking for us,' Amina whispered.

'If he comes next door the first place he'll look will be here.'

'Will Santa know to come here?' Danny asked. His dog was pressed by his side. He looked very small and very frightened. It was his mother's fear, Julie thought. He'd be able to feel it.

'Santa always knows where everyone is,' Rob said, squatting before Danny and scratching Luka's ears. It was intuitive, Julie thought. Danny might well recoil from a hug, but a hug to his dog was pretty much the same thing. 'I promise.'

'He's found us before,' Amina managed, but this time she couldn't stop a sob. 'I can't…we were just…'

'Where are you from?' Rob asked gently, still patting Luka.

'Sri Lanka. We left because of the fighting. My husband… He's a construction engineer. He had a good job; we had a nice house but we… things happened. We had to come here, but here he can't be an engineer. He has to retrain but it's so expensive to get his Australian accreditation. We're working so hard, trying to get the money so he can do the transition course. Meanwhile,

I've been working as a cleaner.' She tilted her chin. 'I work for the firm that cleans this house. My job's good. We couldn't believe it when we were able to rent our house. We thought…this is heaven. But Henry has to work as a fly in, fly out miner. He'll be so worried right now and I'm scared he might have tried to get here. If he's been caught in the fire…'

Rob rose and took her hands. She was close to collapse, weak with terror.

'It won't have happened,' he said firmly, strongly, in a voice that Julie hadn't heard before. It was a tone that said: *don't mess with me; this is the truth and you'd better believe me.* 'They put road blocks in place last night. No one was allowed in. I was the last, and I had to talk hard to be let through. If your husband had come in before the blocks were in place, then he'd be here now. He can't have. He'll be stuck at the block or even further down the mountain. He'll be trying to get to you but he won't be permitted. He'll be safe.'

Danny was looking up at Rob as if he were the oracle on high. 'Papa's stuck down the mountain?'

'I imagine he's eating his dinner right now.'

'Where will he eat dinner?'

'The radio says a school has been opened at

the foot of the mountains. Anyone who can't get home will be staying at the school.'

'Papa's at school?'

'Yes,' Rob said in that same voice that brooked no argument. 'Yes, he is. Eating dinner. Speaking of dinner...how's it coming along?'

'It's brilliant,' Julie said. 'Michelin three star, no less.'

'I don't doubt it,' Rob said, and grinned at her with the same Rob-grin that twisted her heart with pain and with pleasure. 'Do we have enough to give some to Luka?'

'If Luka eats spaghetti he'll get a very red moustache,' Julie said and Danny giggled.

And Julie smiled back at Rob—and saw the same pain and pleasure reflected in his eyes.

CHAPTER SIX

DANNY AND ROB chatted. It was their saving grace; otherwise their odd little dinner would have been eaten in miserable silence. Too much had happened for Julie to attempt to be social.

Amina was caught up in a pool of misery. Julie's heart went out to her but there was little she could do to help.

She pressed her into eating, with limited success, and worried more.

'When's your baby due?' she asked.

'The twentieth of January.' Amina motioned to Danny. 'We were still in the refugee camp when we had Danny. This was supposed to be so different.'

'It is different.'

'Refugees again,' Amina whispered. 'But not even together.'

'You will be soon,' Julie said stoutly, sending a fervent prayer upward. 'Meanwhile we have ice cream.'

'Ice cream!'

'It's an unopened container, not a hint of ice on it,' she said proudly. 'How's that for fore-thought? I must have pre-prepared, four years ago.'

There was an offer too good to refuse. They all ate ice cream and Julie was relieved to see Amina reach for seconds.

There was another carton at the base of the freezer. Maybe they could even eat ice cream for breakfast.

Breakfast... How long would they be trapped here?

'Now can I go next door?' Amina asked as the last of the ice cream disappeared.

Rob grimaced. 'You're sure you don't want me to check and report back?'

'I need to see.'

'Me too,' Danny said and his mother looked at him and nodded.

'Danny's seen a lot the world has thrown at us. And his father would expect him to be a man.'

Danny's chest visibly swelled.

Kids. They were all the same. Wanting to be grown-up.

Wanting to protect their mum?

It should be the other way round. She should have been able to protect...

'Stop it, Jules,' Rob said in his boss-of-the-world voice, and she flinched. Stop it? How could she stop? It was as if the voices in her head were on permanent replay.

'We need to focus on Santa,' he told her, and his eyes sent her a message that belied his smile. 'Moving on.'

Move on. How could she ever? But here there was no choice. Amina was looking at her and so was Danny. Even Luka… No, actually, Luka was looking at the almost empty ice cream container in her hand.

Move on.

'Right,' she said and lowered the ice cream to possibly its most appreciative consumer. 'Danny, you're going to have to wash your dog's face. Spaghetti followed by chocolate ice cream is not a good look. Meanwhile, I'll see if I can find you some sturdy shoes, Amina, and I have a jogging suit that might fit over your bump. It's not the most gorgeous outfit you might like but it's sensible, and Sensible R Us. Let's get the end of this meal cleared up and then go see if the fire's left anything of your house.'

It hadn't left a thing.

A twisted, gnarled washing line. The skeleton of a washing machine. A mass of smouldering timbers and smashed tiles.

Amina stood weeping. Julie held her and Danny's hands as Rob, in his big boots, stomped over the ruins searching for... Anything.

Nothing.

He came back to them at last, his face bleak. 'Amina, I'm sorry.'

'We didn't have much,' Amina said, faltering. 'My sister...she was killed in the bombing. I had her photographs. That was what I most...' She swallowed. 'But we've lost so much before. I know we can face this too. As long as my Henry is safe.'

'That's a hell of a name for a Sri Lankan engineer,' Rob said and Amina managed a smile.

'My mother-in-law dreamed of her son being an Englishman.'

'Will Australian do instead?'

'It doesn't matter where we are—what we have. It's a long time since we dreamed of anything but our family being safe.'

And then she paused.

The silence after the roar of the fire had been almost eerie. The wind had dropped after the front had passed. There was still the crackle of fire, and occasionally there'd be a crash as fire-weakened timber fell, but there'd been little sound for hours.

Now they heard an engine, faint at first but growing closer.

Rob ushered his little group around Amina's

burned car, around the still burning log that lay over their joint driveways and out onto the road. Rob was carrying Danny—much to Danny's disgust, but he had no sensible shoes. And if anyone was to carry him, it seemed okay that his hero should. Thus they stood, waiting, seeing what would emerge out of the smoky haze.

And when it came, inevitably, magically but far too late, it was a fire engine. Big, red, gorgeous.

Julie hadn't realised how tense she'd been until she saw the red of the engine, until she saw the smoke-blackened firefighters in their stained yellow suits. Here was contact with the outside world.

She had a sudden mad urge to climb on the back and hitch a ride, all the way back to Sydney, all the way back to the safety of her office, her ordered financial world.

Ha. As if this apparition was offering any such transport.

'Are you guys okay?' It was the driver, a grim-faced woman in her fifties, swinging out of the cab and facing them with apprehension.

'No casualties,' Rob told her. 'Apart from minor burns on our dog's feet. But we have burn cream. And ice cream. And one intact house.'

'Good for you.' The guys with her were surveying Amina's house and then looking towards their intact house with surprise. 'You managed to save it?'

'It saved itself. We hid in a bunker.'

'Bloody lucky. Can you stay here?'

'Amina's pregnant,' Rob said. 'And her husband will be going out of his mind not knowing if she's safe.'

The woman looked at Amina, noting Danny, noting everything, Julie thought. She had the feeling that this woman was used to making hard decisions.

'We'll put her on the list for evacuation,' she said. 'How pregnant are you?'

'Thirty-six weeks,' Amina whispered.

'No sign of labour?'

'N…no.'

'Then sorry, love, but that puts you down the list. We're radioing in casualties and using the chopper for evacuation, but the chopper has a list a mile long of people with burns, accidents from trying to outrun the fire or breathing problems. And it's a huge risk trying to take anyone out via the road. There's so much falling timber I'm risking my own team being here. Do you have water? Food?'

'We're okay,' Rob told her. 'We have solar power, generators, water tanks, freezers and a stocked pantry. We have plenty of uncontaminated water and more canned food than we know what to do with.'

'Amazing,' the woman told him. 'It sounds like you're luckier than some of the towns that have been in the fire line. We managed to save houses but they're left with no services. Meanwhile, there are houses further up the mountain that haven't been checked. Our job's to get through to them, give emergency assistance and detail evacuation needs for the choppers, but by emergency we're talking life-threatening. That's all we can do—we're stretched past our limits. But we will take your name and get it put up on the lists at the refuge centres to say you're safe,' she told Amina. 'That should reassure your husband. Meanwhile, stay as cool as you can and keep that baby on board.'

'But we have no way of contacting you if anything...happens,' Rob said urgently and the woman grimaced.

'I know and I'm sorry, but I'm making a call here. We'll get the road clear as soon as we can but that'll be late tomorrow at the earliest, and possibly longer. There's timber still actively burning on the roadside. It's no use driving any-one out if a tree's to fall on them, and that's a real risk. You have a house. Your job is to pro-tect it a while longer and thank your lucky stars you're safe. Have as good a Christmas as you can under the circumstances—and make sure that baby stays where it is.'

They watched the fire truck make its cautious way to the next bend and disappear. All of them knew what they were likely to find. It was a subdued little party that picked its way through the rubble and back to the house.

Luka greeted them with dulled pleasure. His paws obviously hurt. Rob had put on burn cream and dressings. They were superficial burns, he reported, but they were obviously painful enough for the big dog to not want to bother his bandages.

Danny lay down on the floor with him, wrapped his arms around his pet's neck and burst into tears.

'My husband wanted a dog to protect us when he was away,' Amina volunteered, and she sounded close to tears herself. 'But Luka's turned into Danny's best friend. Today Luka almost killed him—and yet here I am, thanking everything that Danny still has him. I hope…I hope…'

And Julie knew what she was hoping. This woman had gone through war and refugee camps. She'd be thinking she was homeless once again. With a dog.

Once upon a time as a baby lawyer, Julie had

visited a refugee camp. She couldn't remember seeing a single dog.

'It's okay, Amina,' she told her. 'If you've been renting next door, then you can just rent here instead. This place is empty.'

'But…' Rob said.

'We never use it.' Julie cast him an uncertain glance. 'We live…in other places. I know you have a lot to think about and this will be something you and your husband need to discuss together, but, right now, don't worry about accommodation. You can stay here for as long as you want.'

'But don't…don't *you* need to discuss it with your husband?' Amina asked, casting an uncertain glance at Rob.

Her husband. Rob. She glanced down at the wedding ring, still bright on her left hand. She still had a husband—and yet she hadn't made one decision with him for four years.

'Rob and I don't live together,' she said, and she couldn't stop the note of bleakness she could hear in her own words. 'We have separate lives, separate…homes. So I'm sure you agree, don't you, Rob. This place may as well be used.'

There was a moment's pause. Silence hung, and for a moment she didn't know how it could end. But then… 'It should be a home again,' Rob said. 'Julie and I can't make it one. It'd be great if you and Henry and your children could make it happy again.'

'No decisions yet,' Amina urged. 'Don't promise anything. But if we could... If Henry's safe—' She broke off again and choked on tears. 'But it's too soon for anything.'

Rob went off to check the perimeter with his mop and bucket again. They had a wide area of burned grass between them and any smouldering timber. The risk was pretty much over but still he checked.

Amina and Danny went to bed. There was a made-up guest room with a lovely big bed, but Danny had spotted the racing-car beds. That was where he wanted to sleep—so Amina tugged one racing car closer to the other and announced that she was sleeping there, with her son.

She was asleep almost as her head hit the pillow. Had she slept at all last night? Julie wondered. She thought again of past fighting and refugee camps and all this woman had gone through.

Danny was fast asleep too. He was sharing his car-bed with Luka. Julie stood in the doorway and looked at them, this little family who'd been so close to disaster.

Disaster was always so close...

Get over it, she told herself harshly. *Move on.*

She needed work to distract herself. She needed legal problems to solve, paperwork to do—stuff that had to be done yesterday.

Rob was out playing fireman but there was no need for the two of them to be there. So what was she supposed to do? Go to bed? She wasn't tired or if she was her body wasn't admitting it. She felt weird, exposed, trapped. Standing in her children's bedroom watching others sleep in their beds... Knowing a man who was no longer her husband was out protecting the property...

What to do? What to do?

Christmas.

The answer came as she headed back down the hall. There in the sitting room was her Christmas tree. Was it only last night that she'd decorated it? Why?

And the answer came clear, obvious now as it hadn't been last night. Because Danny needed it. Because they all needed it?

'Will Santa know to come here?' Danny had asked and Rob had reassured him.

'Santa knows where everyone is.'

That had been a promise and it had to be kept. She wouldn't mind betting Danny would be the first awake in the morning. Right now there was a Christmas tree and nothing else.

Santa had no doubt kept a stash of gifts over at Amina's house, but there was nothing left there now except cinders. Amina had been too exhausted to think past tonight.

'So I'm Santa.' She said it out loud.

'Can I share?'

And Rob was in the doorway, looking at the tree. 'I thought of it while I mopped,' he told her. 'We need to play Father Christmas.'

They could. There was a stash from long ago...

If she could bear it.

Of course she could bear it. Did she make her decision based on emotional back story or the real, tomorrow needs of one small boy? What was the choice? There wasn't one. She glanced at Rob and saw he'd come to the same conclusion she had.

Without a word she headed into their bedroom. Rob followed.

She tugged the bottom drawer out from under the wardrobe, ready to climb—even as toddlers the twins had been expert in finding stuff they didn't want them to find. She put a foot on the first drawer and Rob took her by the waist, lifted her and set her aside.

'Climbing's men's work,' he said.

'Yeah?' Unbidden, came another memory. Their town house in the city. Their elderly neighbour knocking on the door one night.

'Please, my kitten's climbed up the elm outside. He can't get down. Will you help?'

The elm was vast, reaching out over the pavement to the street beyond. The kitten was maybe halfway up, mewing pitifully.

'Right,' Rob had said manfully, though Julie had known him well and heard the qualms behind the bravado.

'Let me call the fire brigade,' she'd said and he'd cast her a look of manly scorn.

'Stand aside, woman.'

Which meant twenty minutes later the kitten was safely back in her owner's arms—having decided she didn't like Rob reaching for her, so she'd headed down under her own steam. And Julie had finally called the fire department to help her husband down.

So now she choked, and Rob glowered, but he was laughing under his glower. 'You're supposed to have forgotten that,' he told her. 'Stupid cat.'

'It's worth remembering.'

'Isn't everything?' he asked obliquely and headed up his drawer-cum-staircase.

And then they really had to remember.

The Christmas-that-never-was was up there. Silently, Rob handed it down. There were glove puppets, a wooden railway set, Batman pyjamas. Colouring books and a blow-up paddling pool. A pile of Christmas wrapping and ties they'd been too busy to use until the last moment. The detritus of a family Christmas that had never made it.

Rob put one of the puppets on his too-big hand. It was a wombat. Its two front paws were his thumb and little finger. Its head had the other fingers stuffed into its insides.

The little head wobbled. 'What do you say, Mrs McDowell?' the little wombat demanded in a voice that sounded like a strangled Rob. 'You reckon we can give me to a little guy who needs me?'

'Yes.' But her voice was strained.

'I'm not real,' the little wombat said—via Rob. 'I'm just a bit of fake fur and some neat stitchery.'

'Of course.'

'But I represent the past.'

'Don't push it, Rob.' Why was the past threatening to rise up and choke her?

'I'm not pushing. I'm facing stuff myself. I've been facing stuff alone for so long…' Rob put down his wombat and picked up the Batman pyjamas. 'It hurts. Would it hurt more together than it does separately? That's a decision we need to make. Meanwhile, we bought these too big for the twins and Danny's tiny. These'll make him happy.'

She could hardly breathe. What was he suggesting? That he wanted to try again? 'I...I know that,' she managed but she was suddenly feeling as if she was in the bunker again, cowering, the outside threats closing in.

Dumb. Rob wasn't threatening. He was holding Batman pyjamas—and smiling at her as if he understood exactly how she felt.

I've been facing stuff alone for so long... She hadn't allowed herself to think about that. She hadn't been able to face his hurt as well as hers.

Guilty...and did she need to add *coward* to her list of failings as well?

'Would it have been easier if it all burned?' Rob asked gently and she flinched.

'Maybe. Maybe it would.'

'So why did you come?'

'You know why.'

'Because it's not over? Because they're still with us?' His voice was kind. 'Because we can't escape it; we're still a family?'

'We're not.'

'They're still with me,' he said, just as gently. 'Every waking moment, and often in my sleep as well, they're with me.'

'Yeah.'

'They're not in this stuff. They're in our hearts.'

'Rob, no.' The pain... She hadn't let herself think it. She hadn't let herself feel it. She'd

worked and she'd worked and she'd pushed emotion away because it did her head in.

'Jules, it's been four years. The way I feel...'

'Don't!'

He looked at her for a long, steady moment
and then he looked down at the wombat. And
nodded. Moving on? 'But we can pack stuff up
for Danny?'

'I...yes.'

'We need things for Amina as well.'

'I have...too many things.' She thought of her
dressing table, stuffed with girly things collected
through a lifetime. She thought of the house next
door, a heap of smouldering ash. Sharing was
a no-brainer; in fact Amina could have it all.

'Wrapping paper?' Rob demanded. The emotion was dissipating. Maybe he'd realised he'd
taken her to an edge that terrified her.

'I have a desk full of it,' she told him, grateful to be back on firm ground.

'Always the organised one.' He hesitated.
'Stockings?'

She took a deep breath at that and the edge
was suddenly close again. Yes, they had stockings. Four. Julie, Rob, Aiden, Christopher. Her
mother had embroidered names on each.

But she could be practical. She could do this.
'I'll unpick the names,' she said.

'We can use pillowcases instead.'

'N…no. I'll unpick them.'

'I can help.' He hesitated. 'I need to head out and put a few pans of water around for the wildlife, and then I'm all yours. But, Jules…'

'Mmm?'

'When we're done playing Santa Claus…will you come to bed with me tonight?'

This was tearing her in two. If she could walk away now she would, she thought. She'd walk straight out of the door, onto the road down to the highway and out of here. But that wasn't possible and this man, the man with the eyes that saw everything there was to know, was looking at her. And he was smiling, but his smile had all her pain behind it, and all his too. They had shared ghosts. Somehow, Rob was moving past them. But for her… The ghosts held her in thrall and she was trapped.

But for this night, within the trap there was wriggle room. She'd remove names from Christmas stockings. She'd wrap her children's toys and address them to Danny. She'd even find the snorkel and flippers she had hidden up on the top of her wardrobe. She'd bought them for Rob because she loved the beach, she'd loved taking the boys there and she was…she had been… slowly persuading Rob of its delights.

Did he go to the beach now? What was he doing with his life?

Who knew, and after this night she'd stop wondering again. But on Christmas morning the ghosts would see her stuffing the snorkel and flippers in his stocking. He'd head out into the burned bush with his pails of water so animals wouldn't die and, while he did, she'd prepare him a Christmas.

And the ghosts would see her lie in his arms this night.

'Yes,' she whispered because the word seemed all she could manage. And then, because it was important, she tried for more. 'Yes, please, Rob. Tonight…tonight I'd like to sleep with you once more.'

Christmas morning. The first slivers of light were making their way through the shutters Rob had left closed because there was still fire danger. The air was thick with the smell of a charred landscape.

She was lying cocooned in Rob's arms and for this moment she wanted nothing else. The world could disappear. For this moment the pain had gone, she'd found her island and she was clinging for all she was worth.

He was some island. She stirred just a little, savouring the exquisite sensation of skin against skin—her skin against Rob's—and she felt him tense a little in response.

'Good, huh?'

He sounded smug. She'd forgotten that smugness.

She loved that smugness.

'Bit rusty,' she managed and he choked on laughter.

'Rusty? I'll show you rusty.' He swung up over the top of her, his dark eyes gleaming with delicious laughter. 'I've been saving myself for you for all this time...'

'There's been no one else?'

She shouldn't have asked. She saw the laughter fade, but the tenderness was there still.

'I did try,' he said. 'I thought I should move on. It was a disaster. You?'

'I didn't even try,' she whispered. 'I knew it wouldn't work.'

'So you were saving yourself for me too.'

'I was saving myself for nobody.'

'Well, that sounds a bit bleak. You know, Jules, maybe we should cut ourselves a little slack. Put bleakness behind us for a bit.'

'For today at least,' she conceded, and tried to smile back. 'Merry Christmas.'

'Merry Christmas to you, too,' he said, and the wickedness was back. 'You want me to give you your first present?'

'I...'

'Because I'm about to,' he said and his gorgeous muscular body, the body she'd loved with all her heart, lowered to hers.

She rose to meet him. Skin against skin. She took his body into her arms and tugged him to her, around her, merging into the warmth and depth of him.

Merry Christmas.

The ghosts had backed off. For now there was only Rob, there was only this moment, there was only now.

They surfaced—who could say how much later? They were entwined in each other's bodies, sleepily content, loosely covered by a light cotton sheet. Which was just as well as they emerged to the sound of quiet but desperate sniffs.

Danny.

They rolled as one to look at the door, as they'd done so many times with the twins.

Danny was in the doorway, clutching Luka's collar. He was wearing a singlet and knickers. His hair was tousled, his eyes were still dazed with sleep but he was sniffing desperately, trying not to cry.

'Hey,' Rob said, hauling the sheet a little higher. 'Danny! What's up, mate?'

'Mama's crying,' Danny said. 'She's crying and crying and she won't stop.'

'That'll be because your house is burned and your dad's stuck down the mountain,' Rob said prosaically, as if this was the sort of thing that happened every day. 'I guess your dad won't be able to make it here for a while yet, so maybe it's up to us to cheer her up. What do you think might help?'

'I don't know,' Danny whispered. 'Me and Luka tried to hug her.'

'Hugs are good.' Rob sat up and Julie lay still and watched, trying not to be too conscious of Rob's naked chest, plus the fact that he was still naked under the sheet, and his body was still touching hers and every sense…

No. That was hardly fair because she was tuned to Danny.

She'd been able to juggle…everything when they were a family. She glanced at her watch. Eight o'clock. Four years ago she'd have been up by six, trying to fit in an hour of work before the twins woke. Even at weekends, the times they'd lain here together, they'd always been conscious of pressure.

Yeah, well, both of them had busy professional lives. Both of them thought…had thought…getting on was important.

'You know, hugs are great,' Rob was saying and he lay down again and hugged Julie, just to demonstrate. 'But there might be something better today. Did you remember today is Christmas?'

'Yes, but Mama said Santa won't be able to get through the burn,' Danny quavered. 'She says…Santa will have to wait.'

'I don't think Santa ever waits,' Rob said gravely. 'Why don't you go look under the Christmas tree while Julie and I get dressed? Then we'll go hug your mama and bring her to the tree too.'

'There might be presents?' Danny breathed.

'Santa's a clever old feller,' Rob told him. 'I don't think he'd let a little thing like a bush fire stop him, do you?'

'But Mama said…'

'Your mama was acting on incorrect information,' Rob told him. 'She doesn't know Australia like Julie and I do. Bush fires happen over Australian Christmases all the time. Santa's used to it. So go check, but no opening anything until we're all dressed and out there with you. Promise?'

'I promise.'

'Does Luka promise, too?'

And Danny giggled and Julie thought she did have senses for something—for someone—other than Rob.

To make a child smile at Christmas… It wasn't a bad feeling.

Actually, it was a great feeling. It drove the pain away as nothing else could.

And then she thought…it was like coming out of bleak fog into sunlight.

It was a sliver, the faintest streak of brilliance, but it was something that hadn't touched her for so long. She'd been grey for years, or sepia-toned, everything made two-dimensional, flat and dull.

Right now she was lying in Rob's arms and she was hearing Danny giggle. And it wasn't an echo of the twins. She wasn't thinking of the twins.

She was thinking this little boy had been born in a refugee camp. His mother had coped with coming from a war-torn country.

She'd wrapped the most beautiful alpaca shawl for Amina, in the softest rose and cream. She knew Amina would love it; she just knew.

And there was a wombat glove puppet just waiting to be opened.

'Go,' she ordered Danny, sitting up too, but hastily remembering to keep her sheet tucked around her. 'Check out the Christmas tree and see if Rob's right and Santa's been. I hope he's been for all of us. We'll be there in five minutes, and then we need to get your mama up and tell her things will be okay. And they will be okay, Danny. It's Christmas and Rob and I are here to make sure that you and your mama and Luka have a very good time.'

They did have a good time. Amina was teary but, washed and dressed in a frivolous bath robe Rob had once given Julie, ensconced in the most comfortable armchair in the living room, tears gave way to bemusement.

Julie had wrapped the sensible gifts, two or three each, nice things carefully chosen. Rob, however, had taken wrapping to extremes, deciding there was too much wrapping paper and it couldn't be wasted. So he'd hunted the house and wrapped silly things. As well as the scarf and a bracelet from Africa, Amina's stocking also contained a gift-wrapped hammer, nails, a grease gun—*'because you never know what'll need greasing'*, Rob told her—and a bottle of cleaning bleach. They made Amina gasp and then giggle.

'Santa thinks I might be a handyman?'

'Every house needs one,' Rob said gravely. 'In our house I wear the tool belt but Santa's not sexist.'

'My Henry's an engineer.'

'Then you get to share. Sharing a grease gun—that's real domestic harmony.'

Amina chuckled and held her grease gun like it was gold and they moved on.

Julie's stocking contained the nightdress she'd lusted after four years before and a voucher for a day spa, now long expired. *Whoops*.

'The girls at the spa gift-wrapped it for me four years ago,' Rob explained. 'How was I to know it had expired?' Then, 'No matter,' he said expansively. 'Santa will buy you another.'

He was like a bountiful genie, Julie thought, determined to make each of them happy.

He'd made her happy last night. Was it possible…? Did she have the courage…?

'You have another gift,' Rob reminded her and she hauled her thoughts back to now.

Her final gift was a wad of paper, fresh from their printer. Bemused, she flicked through it.

It was *Freezing—the Modern Woman's Survival Guide,* plus a how-to manual extolling the virtues of ash in compost. He'd clearly got their printer to work while she'd gift-wrapped. He'd practically printed out a book.

She showed Amina and both women dissolved into laughter while Rob beamed benevolently.

'Never say I don't put thought into my gifts,' he told them and Julie held up the spa voucher.

'An out-of-date day spa?'

'They cancel each other out. I still rock.'

They chuckled again and then turned their attention to Danny.

Danny was simply entranced. He loved the

pyjamas and his fire engine but most of all he loved the wombat puppet. Rob demonstrated. Danny watched and was smitten.

And so was Julie. She watched the two of them together and she thought: *I know why I fell in love with this man.*

I know why I love this man?

Was she brave enough to go there?

As well as snorkel and flippers—which Rob had received with open enjoyment before promising Danny that they could try them out in the bath later—Julie had given Rob a coat—a cord jacket. She remembered buying it for him all those years ago. She'd tried it on herself, rushing in her lunch hour, last-minute shopping. It had cost far more than she'd budgeted for but she'd imagined it on Rob, imagined holding him when he was wearing it, imagined how it'd look, faded and worn, years hence.

She should have given it to him four years ago. Now he shrugged himself into it and smiled across the room at her and she realised why she hadn't given it to him. Why she'd refused to have contact with him.

She was afraid of that smile.

Was she still? Tomorrow, would she…?

No. Tomorrow was for tomorrow. For now she needed to watch Danny help Luka open a multi-wrapped gift that finally revealed a packet of biscuits scarily past their use-by date. Oatmeal gingernuts. 'They'll be the closest thing Santa could find to dog biscuits,' Rob told Danny.

'Doesn't Santa have dog biscuits at the North Pole?'

'I reckon he does,' Rob said gravely. 'But I think he'll have also seen all this burned bush and thought of all the animals out here who don't have much to eat. So he might have dropped his supply of dog biscuits out of his sleigh to help.'

'He's clever,' Danny said and Rob nodded. 'And kind.'

He's not the only one, Julie thought, and her heart twisted. Once upon a time this man had been her husband. If she could go back...

Turn back time? As if that was going to happen.

'Is it time to put the turkey on?' Rob asked and Julie glanced at him and thought *he's as tense as I am.* Making love didn't count, she thought, or it did, but all it showed was the same attraction was there that had always been there. And with it came the same propensity for heartbreak.

He was still wearing his jacket. He liked it. You could always tell with Rob. If he loved something, he loved it for ever. And she realised that might just count for her too.

Whether she wanted that love or not.

Switch to practical. 'We still need to use the barbecue,' she said. 'We don't have enough electricity to use the oven.'

'That's us then,' Rob said, puffing his chest. 'Me and Danny. Barbecuing's men's work, hey, Dan?'

'Can my wombat help?'

'Sure he can.'

'I'm not sure what we can have with it,' Julie said. 'There doesn't seem to be a lot of salad in the fridge.'

'Let me look at what you have,' Amina said. 'I can cook.'

'Don't you need to rest?'

'I've had enough rest,' Amina declared. 'And I can't sleep. I need to know my husband's safe. I can't rest until we're all together.'

That's us shot then, Julie thought bleakly. For her family, together was never going to happen.

They ate a surprisingly delicious dinner—turkey with the burned-from-the-freezer bits chopped off, gravy made from a packet mix and couscous with nuts and dried fruit and dried herbs.

They had pudding, slices fried in the butter she'd bought with the bread, served with custard made from evaporated milk.

They pulled bon-bons. They wore silly hats. They told jokes.

But even Danny kept glancing out of the window. He was waiting for his father to appear.

So much could have happened. If he'd tried to reach them last night… All sorts of scenarios were flitting through Julie's mind and she didn't like any of them.

Once catastrophe struck, did you spend the rest of your life expecting it to happen again? Of course you did.

'He'll be fine.' Astonishingly, the reassurance came from Amina. Had she sensed how tense Julie was? 'What you said made sense. He'll be at the road block. And, as for the house… We've seen worse than this before. We'll survive.'

'Of course you will.'

'No, you have to believe it,' Amina said. 'Don't just say it. Believe it or you go mad.'

What had this woman gone through? She had no idea. She didn't want to even imagine.

'I'd like to do something for you,' Amina said shyly. 'If you permit… In the bathroom I noticed a hair colour kit. Crimson. Is it yours?'

'Julie doesn't colour her hair,' Rob said, but Julie was remembering a day long ago, a momentary impulse.

She'd be a redhead for Christmas, she'd thought. Her boys would love it, or she thought they might. But of course she hadn't had time to go to a salon. On impulse she'd bought a do-it-yourself kit, then chickened out at the last minute—of course—and the kit had sat in the second bathroom since.

'I'm a hairdresser,' Amina said, even more shyly. 'In my country, that's what I do. Or did. My husband has to retrain here for engineering but there are no such requirements for hairdressing, and I know this product.' She gazed at Julie's hair with professional interest. 'Colour would look good, but I don't think all over. If you permit, I could give you highlights.'

'I don't think…'

'Jules,' Rob said, and she heard an undercurrent of steel, 'you'd look great with red highlights.'

She'd hardly touched her ash-blonde curls for four years. She tugged them into a knot for work; when they became too unruly to control she'd gone to the cheap walk-in hairdresser near work and she'd thought no more about it.

Even before the boys died… When had she last had time to think about what her hair looked like?

When she'd met Rob she'd had auburn highlights. He'd loved them. He'd played with her curls, running his long, strong fingers through them, massaging her scalp, kissing her as the touch of his fingers through her hair sent her wild…

Even then she hadn't arranged it herself. Her mother had organised it as a gift.

'I bought this voucher for you, pet. I know you don't have time for the salon but you need to make a little time for yourself.'

Her parents were overseas now, having the holiday of a lifetime. They wouldn't be worried about her. They knew she'd be buried in her work.

They'd never imagine she'd be here. With time…

'I don't think…'

'Do it, Jules,' Rob said and she caught a note of steel in his voice. She looked at him uncertainly, and then at Amina, and she understood.

This wasn't about her. Rob wasn't pushing her because he wanted a wife…an cx-wife…with crimson highlights. He was pushing her because Amina needed to do something to keep her mind off her burned house and her missing husband. And she also needed to give something back.

She thought suddenly of the sympathy and kindness she'd received during the months after the boys' deaths and she remembered thinking, more than once: *I want to be the one giving sympathy. I want to give rather than take.*

Amina was a refugee. She would have been needing help for years. Now, this one thing…

'I'd love highlights,' she confessed and Amina

smiled, really smiled, for the first time since she'd met her. It was a lovely smile, and it made Danny smile too.

She glanced at Rob and his stern face had relaxed.

Better to give than receive? Sometimes not. Her eyes caught Rob's and she knew he was thinking exactly the same thing.

He'd have been on the receiving end of sympathy too. And then she thought of all the things he'd tried to make her feel better—every way he could during those awful weeks in hospital, trying and trying, but every time she'd pushed him away.

'Don't get soppy on us,' Rob said, and she blinked and he chuckled and put his arm around her and gave her a fast, hard hug. 'Right, Amina, we need a hair salon. Danny, I need your help. A chair in the bathroom, right? One that doesn't matter if it gets the odd red splash on it.'

He set them up, and then he disappeared. She caught a glimpse of him through the window, heading down to the creek, shovel over his shoulder.

She guessed what he'd be doing. He'd left water for wildlife, but there'd be animals too badly burned...

'He's a good man,' Amina said and she turned

and Amina was watching her. 'You have a good husband.'

'We're not…together.'

'Because of your babies?'

'I…yes.'

'It happens,' Amina said softly. 'Dreadful things…they tear you apart or they pull you together. The choice is yours.'

'There's no choice,' she said, more harshly than she intended, but Danny was waiting in the bathroom eyeing the colouring kit with anticipation, and she could turn away and bite her lip and hope Amina didn't sense the surge of anger and resentment that her words engendered.

Get over it… It was never said, not in so many words, but, four years on, she knew she was pretty much regarded as cool and aloof. The adjectives were no longer seen as a symptom of loss—they simply described who she was.

And who she intended to be for the rest of her life?

Thinking ahead was too hard. But Rob was gone, off to do what he could for injured wildlife, and Danny was waiting in the bathroom and Amina was watching her with a gaze that said she saw almost too much.

Do something.

Back in the office, she'd be neck-deep in contracts.

It was Christmas Day.

Okay, back home, she'd have left her brother's place after managing to stay polite all through Christmas dinner and now she'd be back in her apartment. Neck-deep in contracts.

But now…neck-deep in hair dye?

'Let's get this over with,' she muttered and Amina took a step back.

'You don't have to. If you don't want…'

She caught herself. If Rob came back and found her wallowing in self-pity, with her hair the same colour and Amina left alone…

See, there was the problem. With Rob around she couldn't wallow.

Maybe that was why she'd left him.

Maybe that was selfish. Maybe *grief* was self-ish.

It was all too hard. She caught herself and forced a smile and then tried even harder. This time the smile was almost natural.

'Rob is a good man,' she conceded. 'But he needs a nicer woman than me. A happier one.'

'You can be happier if you try,' Amina told her.

'You can be happy if you have red hair,' Danny volunteered and she grinned at his little-boy answer to the problems of the world.

'Then give me red hair,' she said. 'Red hair is your mum's gift to me for Christmas, and if there's one thing Christmas needs it's gifts. Are you and Luka going to watch or are you going to play with your Christmas presents?'

'Me and Luka are going to watch,' Danny said, and he wiggled his glove puppet. 'And Wombat. Me and Luka and Wombat are going to watch you get happy.'

Almost as soon as they started, Julie realised that agreeing to this had been a mistake.

Putting a colour through her hair would have been a relatively easy task—simply applying the colour, leaving it to take and then washing it out again.

Amina, though, had different ideas. 'Not flat colour,' she said, just as flatly. 'You want highlights, gold and crimson. You'll look beautiful.'

Yeah, well, she might, but each highlight meant the application of colour to just a few strands of hair, then those strands wrapped in foil before Amina moved to the next strands.

It wasn't a job Amina could do sitting down. She also didn't intend to do a half-hearted job.

'If I put too much hair in each foil, then you'll have flat clumps of colour,' she told Julie as she protested. 'It won't look half as good. And I want some of them strong and some diluted.'

'But you shouldn't be on your feet.' She hadn't thought this through. Amina was eight months pregnant, she'd had one hell of a time and now she was struggling.

She looked exhausted. But...

'I need to do this,' Amina told her. 'Please...I want to. I need to do something.'

She did. Julie knew the worry about her husband was still hanging over her, plus the overwhelming grief of the devastation next door. But still...

'I don't want you to risk this baby,' she told her. 'Amina, this is madness.'

'It's not madness,' Amina said stubbornly. 'It's what I want to do. Sit still.'

So she sat, but she worried, and when Rob appeared as the last foil was done she felt a huge wash of relief. Not that there was anything Rob could do to help the situation but at least...at least he was here.

She'd missed him...

'Wow,' Rob said, stopping at the entrance to the bathroom and raising his brows in his grimy face. 'You look like a sputnik.'

'What's a sputnik?' Danny demanded.

'A spiky thing that floats round in space,' Rob told him. 'You think we should put Julie in a rocket launcher and send her to the moon?'

Danny giggled and Amina smiled and once again there was that lovely release of tension that only Rob seemed capable of producing. He was the best man to have in a crisis.

'Amina's exhausted, though,' Julie told him. 'She needs to sleep.'

'You need to keep those foils in for forty minutes,' Amina retorted. 'Then you need a full scalp massage to get the colour even and then a wash and condition. Then I'll rest.'

'Ah, but I'm back now,' Rob said, and Julie knew he could see the exhaustion on Amina's face. He'd have taken in her worry at a glance. 'And if anyone's going to massage my wife it's me. Forty minutes?' He glanced at his watch. 'Amina, I came to ask if there was anything precious, any jewellery, anything that might have survived the fire that you'd like us to search for. The radio's saying it may rain tonight, in which case the ash will turn to concrete. Sputnik and I could have a look now.'

Julie choked. *Sputnik?* She glanced in the mirror. She was wearing one of Rob's shirts, faded jeans, and her head was covered in silver spikes. Okay, yep. Sputnik.

'I could be a Christmas decoration instead,' she volunteered. 'One of those shiny spiky balls you put on top of the tree.'

'You'll be more help sifting through ash. I assume you can put a towel around the spikes—the wildlife has had enough scares for the time being without adding aliens to the mix. Amina, is that okay with you?'

'I will look,' Amina said but Rob caught her hands. He had great hands, Julie thought inconsequentially. He was holding Amina and Julie knew he was imparting strength, reassurance, determination. All those things…

He was a good man. Her husband?

'The ground's treacherous,' he told her. 'Your house is a pile of ash and rubble and parts of it are still very hot. Julie and I have the heavy boots we used to garden in, we have strong protective clothing and we're not carrying a baby. You need to take care of your little one, and of Danny. We won't stay over there for long—it's too hot—but we can do a superficial search. If you tell us where to look…'

'Our bedroom,' Amina told him, meeting his stern gaze, giving in to sense. 'The front bay window…you should see the outline. Our bed started two feet back from the window and was centred on it. The bed was six foot long. On either side of the bed was a bedside table. We each had a box…'

'Wood?' Rob asked without much hope.

'Tin.'

'Well, that's possible. Though don't get your hopes up too much; that fire was searing and tin melts. We'll have a look—but only if you try and get some rest. Danny, will you stand guard while your mum sleeps?'

'I want to help with the burn.'

'There'll be lots of time to help with the burn,' Rob said grimly. 'But, for now, you need to be in charge of your mother. Go lie down beside her, play with your toys while she sleeps, but if she tries to get up, then growl at her. Can you do that?'

Danny considered. 'Because of the baby?'

'Yes.'

'Papa says I have to look after her because of the baby.'

'Then you'll do what your papa asked?'

'Yes,' Danny said and then his voice faltered. 'I wish he'd come.'

'He will come,' Rob said in a voice that brooked no argument. 'He will come. I promise.'

CHAPTER SEVEN

'IT SHOULD HAVE been ours.' Julie stood in the midst of the devastation that was all that was left of Amina's house, she glanced across at their intact home and she felt ill.

'Fire doesn't make sense,' Rob told her, staring grimly round the ruin.

'No. And I understand that it was your design that saved it. But Amina's house was...a home.'

'Our place will be a home again. If we rent it out to them, Amina will make it one. I suspect she's been making homes in all sorts of places for a long time.'

'I know. Home's where the heart is,' Julie said bleakly. 'They all say it. If you only knew how much I hate that saying.'

'We're not here for self-pity, Jules,' Rob said, hauling her up with a start. He sounded angry, and maybe justifiably. This was no time to wallow. 'If it rains, then there'll be little chance of finding anything. Let's get to it.' He handed her a pair of leather gloves and a shovel. 'Watch your feet for anything hot. Sift in front of you before you put your feet down. Don't go near anywhere that looks unstable.'

There wasn't much that looked unstable. The house had collapsed in on itself. The roof was corrugated iron, but Rob must have been here before, because it had been hauled off site.

The bedroom. They could see the outline of the bay window.

'You focus on either side of where the bed would have been,' Rob told her. 'I'm doing a general search.'

What a way to spend Christmas afternoon. Overdressed, hot, struggling to breathe with the wafts of smoke still in the air, her hair in spikes, covered by a towel, squatting, sifting through layer upon layer of warm ash…

She found the first tin almost immediately. It had melted—of course it had—but it had held enough of its shape to recognise it for what it was.

Who knew what was inside? There was no time now to try and open it. She set it aside and moved to the other side of where the bed would have been and kept on searching.

And was stopped in her tracks by a whoop.

She looked up and Rob was standing at the

rear of the house, where the laundry would have been. He'd been shovelling.

'Jules, come and see.'

She rose stiffly and made her way gingerly across the ruin.

It was a safe. Unmistakably it was a safe and it must be fireproof, judging by the fact that it looked intact, even its paintwork almost un-scathed.

'It must have been set in the floor,' Rob said. 'Look, it's still in some sort of frame. But I can get it out.'

'Do you think Amina knew it was there?'

'Who knows? But we'll take it next door. How goes the tin hunt?'

'One down.'

'Then let's find the other.' He grabbed her and gave her a hard unexpected hug. 'See, good things can happen. I just hope there's something inside that safe other than insurance papers.'

'Insurance papers would be good.'

'You and I both know that's not important. And we have five minutes to go before sputnik takes off. Tin, Jules, fetch.'

And, amazingly, they did fetch—two minutes later their search produced a tin box even more melted than the first. Three prizes. Rob brought the barrow from their yard, then they heaved the safe into it and carted it back. 'I feel like a pup with two tails,' Rob said.

Julie grinned and thought: *fun*.

That had been fun. She'd just had fun with Rob. How long since…?

She caught herself, a shaft of guilt hitting her blindside as it always did when she started forgetting. She had no right…

They parked their barrow on the veranda and went to check on Amina. She was fast asleep, as was Danny, curled up beside her. Luka was by their bedside, calmly watchful. The big dog looked up at them as if to say: *What's important enough to wake them up?*

Nothing was. But the foils had to come off.

'I can take them off myself,' Julie said, but dubiously, because in truth they were now overdue to come off and, by the time she took off every last one, the fine foils would be well overdone. What happened if you cooked your hair for too long? Did it fall out? She had no idea, and she had no intention of finding out.

'I'll take them out,' Rob said and looked ruefully down at himself. 'Your beautician, though, ma'am, is filthy.'

'In case you hadn't noticed, your client is filthy too. Can you imagine me popping into a high-class Sydney salon like this?'

'You'd set a new trend,' Rob told her, touching her foils with a grin. 'Smoked Sputnik. It'd take off like a bush fire.'

'Of course it would,' she lied. She'd reached the bathroom now and looked at the mirror. 'Ugh.'

'Let's get these things off then,' he said. 'Sit.'

So she sat on the little white bathroom stool, which promptly turned grey with soot. Rob stood behind her and she watched in the mirror as he slid each foil from her hair.

He worked swiftly, dextrously, intently. He was always like this on a job, she remembered. When he was focused on something he blocked out the world.

When he made love to her, the world might well not exist.

He was standing so close. He smelled of fire, of smoke, of burned eucalyptus. His fingers were in her hair, doing mundane things, removing foils, but it didn't feel mundane. It felt…it felt…

Too soon, the last of the foils was gone, heaped into the trash. Her hair was still spiky, looking very red. Actually, she wouldn't mind if it was green, she thought, as long as she could find an excuse to keep Rob here with her. To stretch out this moment.

'I can…' Her voice wobbled and she fought to steady it. 'I can go from here. I'll shower it off.'

'You need a full scalp massage to even the colour,' Rob told her, but his voice wasn't steady either. It was, however, stern. 'I'm Amina's underling. She's given us orders. The least we can do is obey.'

'I can do it by myself.'

'But you don't have to,' he said, and he bent and touched her forehead with his mouth. It was a feather touch, hardly a kiss, just a fleeting sensation, but it sent shivers through her whole body. 'For now, just give in and forget about facing things alone.'

So she gave in. Of course she did. She sat perfectly still while Rob massaged her scalp with his gorgeous, sensuous fingers and her every nerve ending reacted to him.

He was filthy, covered with smoke and ash. If you met this man on a dark night you'd scream and run, she thought, catching his reflection in the mirror in the split second she allowed herself to glance at him. For she couldn't watch. Feeling him was bad enough…or good enough…

Good was maybe too small a word. Her entire body was reacting to his touch. Any more and she'd turn and take him. She wanted…

'Conditioner,' Rob said, only the faintest tremor cutting through the prosaic word. 'Amina said conditioner.'

'It's in the shower.'

'Then I suggest,' he said, bending down so his lips were right against her ear, 'that we adjourn to the shower.'

'Rob…'

'Mmm?'

'N…nothing.'

'No objections?'

'We…we might lock the door first.'

'What an excellent idea,' he said approvingly. 'I have a practical wife. I always knew I had a practical wife. I'd just forgotten…'

And seemingly in one swift movement the door was locked and she was swept into his arms. He pushed the shower screen back with his elbow and deposited her inside.

It was a large shower. A gorgeous shower. They'd built it…well, they'd built it when they were in love.

It was wide enough for Rob to step inside with her and tug the glass screen closed after them.

'Clothes,' he said. 'Stat?'

'Stat?'

'That's what they say in hospitals in emergencies. Oxygen here, nurse, stat.'

'So we need clothes?'

'We don't need clothes. If this was a hospital and I was a doctor, that's what I'd be saying. Nurse, my wife needs her clothes removed. Stat.'

'Rob…'

'Yes?'

She looked at him and she thought she needed to say she wasn't his wife. She should say she didn't have the courage to take this further. She was too selfish, too armoured, too closed.

But he was inches away from her. He smelled of bush fire. His face was grimy and blackened. As was she.

The only part of her that wasn't grimy or blackened was her hair. Crimson droplets were dripping onto the white shower base, mixing with the ash.

How much colour had Amina put in? How had she trusted a woman she didn't know to colour her hair?

Rob was standing before her, holding her.

She trusted this man with all her heart, and that was the problem. She felt herself falling…

Where was her armour?

She'd find it tomorrow, she told herself. This was an extraordinary situation. This was a time out, pretend, a disaster-induced remarriage that would dissolve as soon as the rest of the world peered in. But for this moment she was stranded in this time, in this place…

In this shower.

And Rob was tugging her shirt up over her head and she was lifting her arms to help him.

And then, as the shirt was tossed over the screen, as he turned his attention to her bra, she started to undo the buttons of his shirt.

Her hands were shaking.

He took her hands in his and held. Tight. Hard. Cupping her hands, completely enfolding them.

'There's no need for shaking, Jules. I'd never hurt you.'

'I might…hurt you.'

'I'm a big boy now,' he told her. 'I can take it.'

'Rob, I need to say…this is for now. I don't think…I still can't think…'

'Of course you can't.' He held her still. 'But for now, for this moment, let's take things as they come. Let our bodies remember why we fell in love. Let's start at the beginning and let things happen.'

And then he kissed her, and that kiss made her forget every other thing. Everything but Rob.

Water was streaming over them. Somehow they managed to stop, pull back, give themselves time to haul their clothes off and toss them out, a sodden, stained puddle to be dealt with later.

Everything could be dealt with later, Julie thought hazily as she turned back to her beautiful naked Rob. For now there was only Rob. There was only this moment.

Water was running in rivulets down his beautiful face, onto his chest, lower. He was wet and glistening and wonderful. His hands were on the small of her back, drawing her into him, and the feel of wet hands on wet skin was indescribably erotic.

For now there was no pain. There was no yesterday. There was only this man, this body. There was only this desire and the only moment that mattered was now.

'You think we should have a nap now, too?' Rob asked.

Somehow they were out of the shower, sated, satisfied, dazed.

Maybe she should make that almost satisfied, Julie thought. Rob was drying her. She was facing the mirror, watching him behind her. The feel of the towel was indescribably delicious.

He pressed her down onto the bathroom stool and started drying her hair. Gently. Wonderfully.

If she could die now, she'd float to heaven. She was floating already.

'If we go anywhere near the bed I can't be held responsible for what happens,' she managed and Rob chuckled. Oh, she remembered that chuckle. She'd forgotten how much she'd missed it.

How much else had she forgotten?

Had she wanted to forget…all of it?

'Maybe you're right. But maybe it's worth not being responsible,' Rob growled. 'But I want to see your hair dry first.'

Her hair. She'd had colour foils put in. Every woman in her right senses regarded the removing of colour foils with trepidation, hoping the colour would work. For some reason Julie had forgotten all about it.

'It looks good wet,' Rob said, stooping and kissing her behind her ear. 'Let's see it dry.'

She tried to look at it in the mirror. Yeah, well, that was a mistake. Rob was right behind her and he was naked. How was a woman to look at her hair when her hairdresser was…Rob?

'I…I can do it,' she tried but he was already hauling the hairdryer from the cabinet. This place was a time warp. Everything had simply been left. It had been stupid, but coming back here four years ago had been impossible. She'd simply abandoned everything…which meant she had a hairdryer.

And, stupid or not, that had its advantages, she decided, as Rob switched on the dryer and directed warm air at her hair. As did the solar panels he'd installed on the roof and the massive bank of power batteries under the house.

They had electricity, and every cent they'd paid for such a massive backup was worth it just for this moment. For the power of one hairdryer.

She couldn't move. Her body seemed more alive than she could remember. Every nerve was tingling, every sense was on fire but she couldn't move. She was paralysed by the touch of his hands, by the warmth of the dryer, by the way he lifted each curl and twisted and played with it as he dried it.

By the way he watched her in the mirror as he dried.

By the way he just…was.

He was lighting her body.

He was also lighting her hair. Good grief, her hair…

It was almost dry now, and the colours were impossible to ignore. They were part of the same magical fantasy that was this moment, but these colours weren't going to go away with the opening of the bathroom door.

What had happened?

She'd bought auburn highlights, but what Amina had done… She must have mixed them in uneven strengths, done something, woven magic…because what had happened *was* magic.

Her mousey-blonde hair was no longer remotely mouse. It was a shiny mass of gold and chestnut and auburn. It was like the glowing embers of a fire, flickering flames on a muted background.

Rob was lifting her curls, watching the light

play on them as he made sure every strand was dry. Her hair felt as if it was their centre. Nothing else mattered.

If only nothing else mattered. If only they could move on from this moment, forgetting everything.

But she didn't want to forget. The thought slammed home and she saw Rob's eyes in the mirror and knew the thought had slammed into him almost simultaneously. They always had known what each other was thinking.

One mind. One body.

'Jules, we could try again,' he said softly, almost as if talking to himself. 'We've done four years of hell. Does it have to continue?'

'I don't see how it can't.'

'We don't have to forget. Going forward together isn't a betrayal. Does it hurt, every time you look at me, because of what we had?'

'No. Yes!'

'I've seen a shrink. There I was, lying on a couch, telling all.' He smiled down at her and lifted a curl, then letting it drop. 'Actually, it was a chair. But the idea's the same. I'm shrunk.'

'And what did he…she…tell you?'

'She didn't tell me anything. She led me round and round in circles until I figured it out. But finally I did. Four people weren't killed that day, though they can be if we let them.'

'You can live…without them?'

'There's no choice, Jules,' he said, his voice suddenly rough. 'Look at us. It's Christmas, our fourth Christmas without them, yet it's all about two little boys who are no longer here. Out there is a little boy who's alive and who needs us to make him happy. We can help Amina be happy, at least for the day. We can do all sorts of things, make all sorts of people happy if we forget we're the walking dead.'

'I'm not…'

'No. You're not the walking dead. Look at your hair. This is fun hair, fantastic hair, the hair of a woman who wants to move forward. And look at your body. It's a woman's body, Jules, your body, and it gives you pleasure. It still can give you pleasure. Maybe it could even give you another child.'

'No!'

'Are you so closed?'

'Are you? You said you've been seeing other women?'

'I said I've been trying,' he said, and once again his fingers started drifting in her curls. 'The problem is they're not you.'

'You can't still love me.'

'I've never stopped.'

'But there's nothing left to love.' She was sounding desperate, negative, harsh. She'd built up so much armour and he'd penetrated it. It was cracking and she was fighting desperately to retain it. If it shattered...how could she risk such hurt again? She felt as if she was on the edge of an abyss, about to fall.

'Jump,' Rob said softly. 'I'll catch you.'

But she had to keep trying. She had to make him see. 'Rob, there are so many women out there. Undamaged. Women who could give you a family again.'

'Are you offering me up for public auction? I'm not available,' he said, more harshly still. 'Julie, remember the first time we came here? Deciding to camp? Me nobly giving you our only single air bed, then the rain at two in the morning and you refusing to move because you were warm and dry and floating?'

'I did move in the end.'

'Only because I tipped you off into six inches of water.'

'That wasn't exactly chivalrous.'

'Exactly. The thing is, Jules, that with you I've never felt the need to be chivalrous. What happens between us just...happens.'

'You did rescue the kitten...sort of.'

'That's what comes of playing the hero. You end up laughing.'

'I didn't laugh at you.'

'No,' he said and he stooped and took her

hands in his. 'You laugh with me. Every time I laugh, I know you're laughing too. And every time I'm gutted it's the same. That's what's tearing me apart the most. I've known, these last four years, that you haven't been laughing. Nor have you been gutted because I would have felt it. You've just been frozen. But I want you, Jules. I want my lovely, laughing Julie back again. We've lost so much. Do we have to lose everything?'

He was so close. His hands enfolded hers. It would be so easy to fall…

But it was easier to make love to him than what he was asking her now. She remembered that closeness. That feeling that she was part of him. That even when he drove her crazy she understood why, and she sort of got that she might be driving him crazy too.

They'd fought. Of course they'd fought. Understanding someone didn't mean you had to share a point of view and often they hadn't.

She'd loved fighting with him and often she hadn't actually minded losing. A triumphant Rob made her laugh.

But to start again…

Could she?

She so wanted to, but…but…

She was like the meat she had taken out from the freezer, she thought tangentially. On the surface she was defrosting but at her core there was still a deep knot of frozen.

If she could get out of here, get away from Rob, then that core would stay protected. Her outer layers could freeze again as well.

Was that what she wanted?

'Jules, try,' Rob said, drawing her into his arms and holding her. 'You can't waste all that hair on legal contracts. Waste it on me.'

'What do you think I'm doing now?'

'But long-term? After the fire.'

'I don't know.' The panic was suddenly back, all around her—the panic that had overwhelmed her the first time she'd walked into the twins' empty bedroom, the panic that threatened to bring her down if she got close to anyone. The abyss was so close...

'I won't push you,' Rob said.

'So making love isn't pushing?'

'That wasn't me,' he said, almost sternly. 'It was both of us. You know you want me as much as I want you.'

'I want your body.'

'You want all of me. You want the part that wants to be part of you again. The part that wants to love you and demands you love me back.'

'Rob...I can't!' How could she stop this overwhelming feeling of terror? She wanted this man so much, but…but…

She had to make one last Herculean effort. One last try to stay…frozen.

'It's…time to get dressed,' she managed, and he nodded and lifted his fingers through her curls one last time.

'I guess,' he said ruefully, achingly reluctant. 'But let's try. Let the world in, my Julie. Let Amina see what her magic produced.'

'Only it's not magic,' she whispered. 'We can't cast a happy-ever-after spell.'

'We could try.'

'We could destroy each other.'

'More than we already have?' He sighed. 'But it's okay. Whatever you decide has to be okay. I *will not* push.' He kissed her once again, on the nape of her neck, and it was all she could do not to turn and take him into her arms and hold him and hold him and hold him. She didn't. The panic was too raw. The abyss too close.

But he was twisting a towel around his hips. It nearly killed her to see his nakedness disappear. If the world wasn't waiting…

Someone was banging on the front door. Luka started barking.

The world was indeed waiting. It was time to dress. It was time to move on.

* * *

Rob reached the front door first. He'd hauled jeans on and left it at that. Amina and Danny must be still asleep, or waking slowly, because only Luka was there, barking hysterically.

The knocking started again as he reached the hall, but for some reason his steps slowed.

He didn't want the world to enter?

Maybe there was a truck outside, emergency personnel offering to take them down the mountain, evacuate them to safety. The authorities would want everyone off the mountain. This place was self-sufficient but most homes were dependent on essential services. That first truck had been the precursor to many. The army could even have been called in, with instructions to enforce evacuation.

He didn't want to go.

Well, that was dumb. For a start, Amina desperately needed evacuation. It wasn't safe for an eight months pregnant woman to be here, with no guaranteed way out if she went into labour. With the ferocity of the burn and the amount of bushland right up to the edges of the roads, normal traffic would be impossible for weeks. So many burned trees, all threatening to fall… They needed to get out as soon as it was safe to go.

And yet…and yet…

And yet he didn't want to leave.

Maybe he could send Amina and Danny away and keep Julie here.

As his prisoner? That was another dumb thought. He couldn't keep her against her will, nor would he want to, but, even so, the thought was there. The last twenty-four hours had revealed his wife again. He knew she was still hurting. He knew that breaking down her armour required a miracle, and he also knew that once they were off the mountain, then that miracle couldn't happen. She'd retreat again into her world of finance and pain.

'She has to deal with it in her own time.' The words of his shrink had been firm. *'Rob, you've been wounded just as much as she has, but you're working through it. For now it's as much as you can do to heal yourself. You need to let Julie go.'*

But what if they could heal together? These last hours had shown him Julie was still there—the Julie he'd loved, the Julie he'd married.

But he couldn't lock her up. That wasn't the way of healing and he knew it.

What was? Holding her close? She'd let him do that. They'd made love, they'd remembered how their bodies had reacted to each other, yet it had achieved…nothing.

Could he keep trying? Dare he? These last

years he'd achieved a measure of peace and acceptance. Would taking Julie to him open the floodgates again? Would watching her pain drive him back to the abyss? Only he knew how hard it had been to pull himself back to a point where he felt more or less at peace.

He knew what his shrink would say. *Move away and stay away. Leave the past in the past.*

Only the past was in their shared bedroom, with hair that glistened under his hands, with eyes that smiled at him with…hope? If he could find the strength… If, somehow, he could drag her to the other side of the nightmare…

Enough of the introspection. The knocking continued and he'd reached the door. He tugged it open, Luka launched himself straight out—and into the arms of a guy standing on the doorstep.

The man was shorter than Rob, and leaner. He looked in his forties, dark-skinned and filthy. He looked…haggard. His eyes were bloodshot and he hadn't shaved for a couple of days. He was leaning against the door jamb, breathing heavily, but as Luka launched himself forward he grabbed him and held him as if he was drowning.

He met Rob's eyes over Luka's great head, and his look was anguished.

'Amina?' It was scarcely a croak.

'Safe,' Rob said quickly. 'And Danny. They're both here. They're safe. You're Henry?' He had to be. No one but Amina's husband could say her name with the same mix of love and terror.

'Yes. I am. I went…next door. Oh, God, it's…'

'We got them here before the house went up,' Rob said, speaking quickly, cutting through Henry's obvious terror. 'They're tired but well. They're asleep now but they've been as worried about you as you seem to be about them. They're safe.'

The man's knees sagged. Rob grabbed the dog and hauled him back, then took Henry's elbows under his hands, holding him up. He looked beyond exhaustion.

'They're safe,' he said again. 'I promise. Happy Christmas, Henry. I know your house is burned and I'm sorry, but things can be replaced. People can't. Everything else can wait. For now, come in and see your wife.'

And Henry burst into tears.

After that things seemed to happen in a blur.

There was a whimper behind him. Rob turned and Amina was there, staring in incredulity. And then somehow she was in Rob's place, holding her husband, holding and holding. Weeping.

And then Danny, flying down the hall. 'Papa…' He was between them, a wriggling, excited bundle of joy. 'My Papa's come,' he yelled to anyone who'd listen and then he was between them, sandwiched, muffled but still yelling. 'Papa, our house burned and burned and Luka was lost and I was scared but Rob found me and then we hid in a little cave and we've been here for lots and lots and Santa came and we had turkey but we didn't have chocolates. Mama had them for us but they've been burned as well, but Mama says we can get some more. Papa, come and see my presents.'

Rob backed away and then Julie was beside him, in her gorgeous crimson robe with her gorgeous crimson hair, and she was sniffing. He took her hand and held and it felt…right.

They finally found themselves in the kitchen, watching Henry eat leftover Christmas lunch like he hadn't eaten for a week—but he still wasn't concentrating on the food. He kept looking from Amina to Danny and back again, like he couldn't get enough of them. Like he was seeing ghosts…

His plane last night, a later one than Rob's, had been diverted—landing in Melbourne instead of Sydney because of the smoke. He'd spent the night trying to get any information he could, going crazy because he couldn't contact anyone.

This morning he'd flown into Sydney at

dawn, hired a car, hit the road blocks, left the car, dodged the road blocks and walked.

It didn't take any more than seeing his smoke-stained face and his bloodshot eyes to tell them how fraught that walk had been. And how terror had stayed with him every inch of the way.

But he was home. He had his family back again. Julie watched them with hungry eyes, and Rob watched Julie and thought that going back was a dream. A fantasy. He couldn't live with that empty hunger for ever.

'We've plenty of water. Go and take a bath,' he told Henry, and Danny brightened.

'Luka and I will help,' he announced and they disappeared towards the bathroom, with the sounds of splashing and laughter ensuing. Happy ever after...

'I'll go get dressed,' Julie said, sounding subdued, and Amina touched her hair.

'Beautiful.'

'Yes. Thank you.'

'Don't waste it,' Amina said sternly with a meaningful glance at Rob, and Julie flinched a little but managed a smile.

'I promise I won't wear a hat for months.'

Which wasn't what Amina had meant and they all knew it but it was enough for Julie to escape.

Which left Amina with Rob.

'You love her still,' she said, almost as if she was talking of something mundane, chatting about the weather, and Rob had to rerun the words in his mind for a bit before he could find an answer.

'Yes,' he said at last. 'But our grief threatened to destroy us. It's still destroying us.'

'You want…to try again?'

'I don't think we can.'

'It takes courage,' she whispered. 'So much courage. But you…you have courage to spare. You saved my son.'

'It takes more than courage to wake up to grief every morning of your life.'

'It's better than walking away,' she said softly. 'Walking away is the thing you do when all else fails. Walking away is the end.'

'Amina…'

'I shall cook dinner,' she announced, moving on. 'Food is good. Food is excellent. When all else fails, eat. I need to inspect this frozen-in-time kitchen of yours.'

'You need to rest.'

'I have rested,' she said. 'I have my husband back. My family is together and that's all that matters. We need to move on.'

Christmas dinner was a sort of Middle Eastern goulash made with leftover turkey, couscous, dried herbs, packet stock and raisins. It should have tasted weird—half the ingredients were well over their use-by dates—but it tasted delicious. The house had a formal dining room but no one was interested in using it. They squashed round the kitchen table meant for four, with Luka taking up most of the room underneath, and it felt right.

Home, Rob thought as he glanced at his dinner companions. That was what this felt like. Outside, the world was a bleak mess but here was food, security, togetherness.

Henry couldn't stop looking at Amina and Danny. From one to the other. It was like he was seeing a dream.

That was what looking at Julie felt like too, Rob thought. A dream. Something that could never be.

But still… Henry had made a quick, bleak foray across to the ruins of his house and came back grimly determined.

'We can build again,' he'd said. 'We've coped with worse than this.'

Building again… Could he and Julie? A building needed foundations, though, Rob thought, and their foundations hardly existed any more. At least, that was what Julie thought. She thought their foundations were a bed of pain, of nightmares. Could he ever break through to foundations that had been laid long before the twins were born?

Did he have the strength to try?

'You have our safe,' Henry said as the meal came to an end and anxiety was in his voice again. 'You said you managed to haul it out.'

'I did,' Rob told him. 'I'm not sure whether the contents have withstood the fire.'

'It's built to withstand an inferno. And the contents…it's not chocolate.'

'I'd like some chocolate,' Danny said wistfully, but there was ice cream. Honestly, wrapped containers might cope with a nuclear blast, Rob thought as they sliced through the layers of plastic to ice cream that looked almost perfect.

But Amina didn't want any. She was looking exhausted again. Julie was watching her with concern, and Rob picked up on it.

'You want to go back to bed?' he asked her. 'All of you. Henry's had a nightmare twenty-four hours and you've made us a feast of a Christmas dinner. You've earned some sleep.'

'I'm fine,' Amina said, wincing a little. 'I just have a backache. I need a cushion, that's all.'

In moments she had about four and they moved into the living room, settled in the comfortable lounge suite…wondering where to go from here.

He'd quite like to carry Julie back to the bedroom, Rob thought. It was Christmas night. He could think of gifts he'd like to give and receive...

But Danny had slept this afternoon, and he was wide awake now. He was zooming back and forth across the floor with his new fire truck. In Danny's eyes, Christmas was still happening. There was no way he was going calmly to bed, and that meant the adults had to stay up.

Henry was exhausted. He'd slumped into his chair, his face still grey with exhaustion and stress.

Amina also looked stressed. The effort of making dinner had been too much for her. She had no energy left.

Rob sank to the floor and started playing with Danny, forming a makeshift road for his fire engine, pretending the TV remote was a police car, conducting races, making the little boy laugh. Doing what he'd done before...

It nearly killed her. He was doing what she'd seen him do so many times, what she'd loved seeing him do.

Now he was playing with a child who wasn't his.

He was *getting over it*?

Get over it. How many times had those words

been said to her? 'It'll take time but you will get over it. You will be able to start again.'

She knew she never would, but Rob just might. It had been a mistake, coming back here, she thought. Connecting with Rob again. Reminding themselves of what they'd once had.

It had hurt him, she thought. It had made him hope…

She should cut that hope off right now. There was no chance she could move on. The thought of having another child, of watching Rob romp with another baby… It hurt.

Happy Christmas, she thought bitterly. This was worse than the nothing Christmases she'd had for the last few years. Watching Rob play with a child who wasn't his.

She glanced up and saw Amina was watching her and, to her surprise, she saw her pain reflected in the other woman's eyes.

'Are you okay?' she asked. 'Amina…?'

'It's only the backache,' she said, but somehow Julie knew it wasn't. 'Henry, the safe… Could you check? I need to know.'

'I'll do it in the morning,' Henry said uneasily but Amina shook her head.

'I need to see now. The television…does it work?'

'We have enough power,' Rob told her. 'But there won't be reception.'

'We don't need reception. I just need to see...'

'Amina, it'll hurt,' Henry said.

'Yes, but I still need to see,' she said stubbornly. 'Henry, do this for me, please. I need to see that they're still there.'

Which explained why, ten minutes later, Rob and Henry were out on the veranda, staring at a fire-stained safe. The paint had peeled and charred, but essentially it looked okay.

'Do you want to open it in privacy?' Rob asked, but Henry shook his head.

'We have nothing of value. This holds our passports, our insurance—our house contents are insured, how fortunate is that?'

'Wise.'

'The last house we lost was insured too,' Henry said. 'But not for acts of war.'

'Henry...'

'No matter. This is better. But Amina wants her memories. Do you permit?'

He wasn't sure what was going on but, two minutes later, Henry had worked the still operational combination lock and was hauling out the contents.

Papers, documents...and a couple of USB sticks.

'I worried,' Henry said. 'They're plastic but they seem okay. It would break Amina's heart to lose these. Can we check them on your television?'

'Of course. Julie and I can go to bed if you want privacy.'

'If it's okay with you,' Henry said diffidently, 'it's better to share. I mean…Amina needs to… well, her history seems more real to her if she can share. Right now she's hurting. It would help…if you could watch. I know it'll be dull for you, other people's memories, but it might help. The way Amina's looking… Losing our house. Worrying about me. The baby… It's taken its toll.'

'Of course we can watch.' It was Julie in the doorway behind them. 'Anything that can help has to be okay by us.'

The television worked. The USB worked. Ten minutes later they were in Sri Lanka.

In Amina and Henry's past lives.

The files contained photographs—many, many photographs. Most were amateur snaps, taken at family celebrations, taken at home, a big, assorted group of people whose smiles and laughter reached out across distance and time.

And, as Julie watched her, the stress around Amina's eyes faded. She was introducing people as if they were here.

'This is my mother, Aisha, and my older sister Hannah. These two are my brothers. Haija is an architect like you, Rob. He designs offices, wonderful buildings. The last office he designed had a waterfall, three storeys high. It wasn't built, but, oh, if it had been… And here are my nieces and nephews. And Olivia…' She was weeping a little but smiling through tears as the photograph of a teenage girl appeared on the screen, laughing, mocking the camera, mischief apparent even from such a time and distance. 'My little sister Olivia. Oh, she is trouble. She'll be trouble still. Danny, you remember how I told you Olivia loves trains?' she demanded of her son. 'Olivia had a train set, a whole city. She started when she was a tiny child, wanting and wanting trains. "What are you interested in those for?" my father asked. "Trains are for boys." But Olivia wanted and wanted and finally he bought her a tiny train and a track, and then another. And then our father helped her build such a city. He built a platform she could raise to the roof on chains whenever my mother wanted the space for visitors. Look, here's a picture.'

And there they were—trains, recorded on video, tiny locomotives chugging through an Alpine village, with snow-covered trees and tiny figures, railway stations, tunnels, mountains, little plastic figures, a businessman in a bowler hat endlessly missing his train…

Danny was entranced but he'd obviously seen it before. 'Olivia's trains,' he said in satisfaction and he was right by the television, pointing to each train. 'This green one is her favourite. Mama's Papa gave it to her for her eighth birthday. Mama says when I am eight she'll try and find a train just like that for me. Isn't it lucky I'm not eight yet? If Mama had already found my train, it would have been burned.'

'Do you…still see them?' Rob asked cautiously.

Amina smiled sadly and shook her head. 'Our house was bombed. Accidentally, they said, but that's when Henry and I decided to come here. It's better here. No bombs.'

'Bush fires, though,' Rob said, trying for a smile and, amazingly, Amina smiled back at him, even as she put her hand to her obviously aching back.

'We can cope with what we have to cope with,' she said simply. She looked back at the television to where her sister was laughing at her father. Two little steam engines lay crashed on their side on the model track, obviously victims of a fake disaster. 'You get up and keep going,' she said simply. 'What choice is there?'

You can close down, Julie thought. *You can roll into a tight ball of controlled pain, unbend-*

ing only to work. That was what she'd done for four long years.

'Would you like to see our boys?' Rob asked and her eyes flew wide. What was he saying? Shock held her immobile and it was as if his voice was coming from the television, not from him. But, 'I'd like to show you our sons,' he was saying. 'They're not here either, but they're still in our hearts. It'd be great to share.'

No. No! She wanted to scream it but she couldn't.

'Would you like us to see them, Julie?' Amina asked shyly, tentatively, as if she guessed Julie's pain. As she must. She'd lost so much herself.

'We lost our boys in a car accident four years ago,' Rob told Henry. 'But it still feels like they're here.'

'But it hurts Julie?' Amina said. 'To talk about them? To see them? Is it better not?'

Yes, Julie thought. *Much better.* But then she looked at Rob, and with a shock she realised that his face said it wasn't better at all.

His expression told her that he longed to talk about them. He longed to show these strangers pictures of his sons, as they'd shown him pictures of their family.

'It's up to Jules, though,' Rob said. 'Julie, do you know where the disc is of their birthday?'

She did, but she didn't want to say. She never

spoke of the boys. She never looked at their photographs. They were locked inside her, kept, hers. They were dead.

'Maybe not,' Amina said, still gently. 'If Julie doesn't want to share, that's her right.'

Share…share her boys… She wanted to say no. She wanted to scream it because the thought almost blindsided her. To talk about them…to say their names out loud…to act as if they still had a place in her life…

To see her boys on the screen…

'Jules?' Rob said gently and he crossed the room and stooped and touched her chin with his finger. 'Up to you, love. Share or not? No pressure.'

But it was pressure, she thought desperately, and it was as if the pressure had been building for years. The containment she'd held herself in was no longer holding.

To share her boys… To share her pain…

Rob's gaze was on her, calmly watchful. Waiting for the yay or nay.

No pressure.

Share… Share with this man.

A photo session, she thought. That was all he was asking. To see his kids as they'd been when they'd turned two. How hard was that?

'Don't do it if it hurts,' Amina whispered and

Julie knew that it would hurt. But suddenly she knew that it'd hurt much more not to.

They were her boys. Hers and Rob's. And Rob was asking her to share memories, to sit in this room and look at photographs of their kids and let them come to life again, if only on the screen. To introduce them, to talk of them as Amina had talked of her family.

'I...I'll get it,' she said and Rob ran a finger the length of her cheek. His eyes said he did understand what he was asking, and yet he was still asking.

His gaze said he knew her hurt; he shared it. He shared...

She rose and she staggered a little, but Rob was beside her, giving her a swift, hard hug. 'I love that video,' he said but she knew he hadn't seen it for four years. It had been hidden, held here in limbo. Maybe it was time...

She couldn't think past that. She gave Rob a tight hug in return and went to fetch the disc.

And there they were. Her boys. It had been the most glorious birthday party, held here on the back lawn. All the family had been here—her parents, Rob's parents, their siblings, Rob's brother's kids, Rob's parents' dog, a muddle of family and chaos on the back lawn.

A brand-new paddling pool. Two little boys,

gloriously happy, covered in the remains of birthday cake and ice cream, squealing with delight. Rob swinging them in circles, a twin under each arm.

Julie trying to reach Aiden across the pool, slipping and sprawling in the water. Julie lying in the pool in her jeans and T-shirt, the twins jumping on her, thinking she'd meant it, squealing with joy. Rob's laughter in the background. Julie laughing up at the camera, hugging her boys, then yelling at Rob's dad because the dog was using the distraction to investigate the picnic table.

The camera swivelled to the dog and the remains of the cake—and laughter and a dog zooming off into the bushes with half a cake in his mouth.

Family…

She'd thought she couldn't bear it. She'd thought she could never look at photographs again, but, instead of crying, instead of withering in pain, she found she was smiling. Laughing, even. When the dog took off with the cake they were all laughing.

'Luka wouldn't do that,' Danny decreed. 'Bad dog.'

'They look…like a wonderful family,' Amina said and Rob nodded.

'They are.'

They were. She'd never let them close. She'd seen her remaining family perfunctorily for the last four years, when she had to, and she'd never let anyone talk of the boys.

'Aiden and Christopher were…great.'

She said their names now out loud and it was like turning a key in a rusty lock. She hadn't said their names to anyone else since…

'They're the best kids,' Rob said, smiling. He was gripping her hand, she realised, and she hadn't even noticed when he'd taken it. 'They were here for such a short time, but the way they changed our lives… You know, in the far reaches of my head, they're still with me. When I get together with my parents and we talk about them, they're real. They're alive. I understand why you need your family tonight, Amina. For the same reason I need mine.'

Julie listened, and Rob's words left her stunned. His words left her in a limbo she didn't understand. Like an invitation to jump a crevice…but how could she?

The recording had come to an end. The last frame was of the twins sitting in their pool, beaming out at all of them. She wanted to reach out and touch them. She felt as if her skin was bursting. That she could look at her boys and laugh… That she could hold Rob's hand and remember how it had felt to be a family…

'Thank you for showing us,' Henry said, gravely now, and Julie thought that he knew. This man knew how much it hurt. He'd lost too, him and Amina, but now he was tugging his wife to her feet, holding her...moving on.

'We need to sleep,' he said. 'All of us. But thank you for giving us such a wonderful, magical Christmas. Thank you for saving my family, and thank you for sharing yours.'

They left.

Rob flicked the television off and the picture of their boys faded to nothing.

Without a word, Rob went out to the veranda. He stood at the rail and stared into the night and, after a moment's hesitation, Julie followed. The smouldering bushland gave no chance of starlight but, astonishingly, a few of the solar lights they'd installed along the garden paths still glowed. The light was faint but it was enough to show a couple of wallabies drinking deeply from the water basins Rob had left.

'How many did you put out?' Julie said inconsequentially. There were so many emotions coursing through her she had no hope of processing them.

'As many containers as I could find. I suspect our veranda was a refuge. There are droppings all over the south side. All sorts of droppings.'

'So we saved more than Amina and Danny and Luka.'

'I think we did. It's been one hell of a Christmas.' He hesitated. 'So…past Christmases… Julie, each Christmas, each birthday and so many times in between, I've tried to ring. You know how often, but I've always been sent straight through to voicemail. I finally accepted that you wanted no contact, but it hasn't stopped me thinking of you. I've thought of you and the boys every day. But at Christmas…for me it's been a day to get through the best way I can. But, Julie, how has it been for you? I rang your parents. The year after…they said you were with them but you didn't want to talk to me. The year after that they were away and I couldn't contact you.'

How to tell him what she'd been doing? The first year she'd been in hospital and Christmas had been a blur of pain and disbelief. The next her parents had persuaded her to spend with them.

Doug and Isabelle were lovely ex-hippy types, loving their garden, their books, their lives. They'd always been astonished by their only daughter's decision to go into law and finance, but they'd decreed anything she did was okay by them. Doug was a builder, Isabelle taught disadvantaged kids and they accepted everyone. They'd loved Rob and their grandsons but, after the car crash, they'd accepted Julie's decision that she didn't want to talk of them, ever.

But it had left a great hole. They were so careful to avoid it, and she was so conscious of their avoidance. That first Christmas with them had been appalling.

The next year she'd given them an Arctic cruise as a Christmas gift. They'd looked at her with sadness but with understanding and ever since then they'd travelled at Christmas.

And what had Julie been doing?

'I work at Christmas,' she said. 'I'm international. The finance sector hardly closes down.'

'You go into work?'

'I'm not that sad,' she snapped, though she remembered thinking if the entire building hadn't been closed and shut down over Christmas Day she might have. 'I have Christmas dinner with my brother. But I do take contracts home. It takes the pressure off the rest of the staff, knowing someone's willing to take responsibility for the urgent stuff. How about you?'

'That's terrible.'

'How about you?' she repeated and she made no attempt to block her anger. Yeah, Christmas was a nightmare. But he had no right to make her remember how much of a nightmare it normally was, so she wasn't about to let him off the hook. 'While I've been neck-deep in legal negotiations, what have you been doing?'

'To keep Santa at bay?'

'That's one way of looking at it.'

'I've skied.'

It was so out of left field that she blinked. 'What?'

'Skied,' he repeated.

'Where?'

'Aspen.'

She couldn't have been more astounded if he'd said he'd been to Mars. 'You hate the cold.'

'I hated the cold. I'm not that Rob any more.'

She thought about that for a moment while the stillness of the night intensified. The smell of the smoke was all-consuming but…it was okay. It was a mist around them, enveloping them in a weird kind of intimacy.

Rob in the snow at Christmas.

Without her.

Rob in a life without her.

It was odd, she thought numbly. She'd been in a sort of limbo since the accident, a weird, desolate space where time seemed to stand still. There was no future and no past, simply the piles of legal contracts she had in front of her. When she'd had her family, her work had been important. When she hadn't, her work was everything.

But, meanwhile, Rob had been doing…other stuff. Skiing in Aspen.

'Are you any good?' she asked inconsequentially and she heard him smile.

'At first, ludicrous. A couple of guys from work asked me to go with them. I spent my first time on the nursery slopes, watching three-year-olds zoom around me. But I've improved. I pretty much threw my heart and soul into it.'

'Even on Christmas Day?'

'On Christmas Day I pretty much have the slopes to myself. I ski my butt off, to the point where I sleep.'

'Without nightmares?'

'There are always nightmares, Jules,' he said gently. 'Always. But you learn to live around them.'

'But this Christmas—you didn't go to Aspen?'

'My clients finished the house to die for in the Adelaide Hills. They were having a Christmas Eve party. My sister asked me to join her tribe for Christmas today. I'd decided…well, I'd decided it was time to stay home. Time to move on.'

Without me? She didn't say it. It was mean and unfair. She'd decided on this desolate existence. Rob was free to move on as best he could. But…but…

He was right here, in front of her. Rob. Her

beloved Rob, who she'd turned away from. She could have helped…

Or she could have destroyed him.

He reached out and touched her cheek, a feather touch, and the sensation sent shivers through her body. *Her Rob.*

'Hell, Julie, how do we move on from this?' His voice was grave. Compassionate. Loving?

'I don't know,' she whispered. 'I can't think how to escape this fog.'

There was a moment's hesitation and then his voice changed. 'Escape,' he said bitterly. 'Is that what you want? Do you think Amina was escaping by coming here?'

'I don't know.'

'Well, I do,' he said roughly, almost angrily. 'She wasn't escaping. She was regrouping. Figuring out how badly she and her family had been wounded, and how to survive. And look at her. After all she's been through, back she goes, to her memories, to talking about the ones she loves. You know why I wasn't going to Aspen this Christmas? Because I've finally figured it out. I've finally figured that's what I want, Jules. I want to be able to talk about Aiden and Christopher without hurting. Call it a Christmas list if you want, my Santa wish, but that wish has been with me for four years. Every day I wake up and I want the same thing. I want people to talk of Christopher and Aiden like Amina does of her family. I want to admit that Christopher bugged me when he whined for sweets. I want to remember that Aiden never wanted me to go the bathroom by myself. I want to be able to say that you sometimes took all the bedcovers…'

'I did not!'

'And the one time I got really pissed off and pinned them to my side of the bed you ripped them. You did, too.'

'Rob!'

'Don't sound so outraged.' But then he gave a rueful smile and shrugged. 'Actually, that's okay. Outrage is good. Anything's good apart from silence. Or fog. We've been living with silence for years. Does it have to go on for ever?'

'I'm…safe where I am.'

'Because no one talks about Aiden or Christopher? Or me. Do they talk about me, Julie, or am I as dead to you as the boys are?'

'If they did talk…it hurts.'

But he was still angry. Relentless. The gentle, compassionate Rob was gone. 'Do you remember the first time we climbed this mountain?' he demanded, and he grabbed her hand and hauled her round so she was facing out to where the smoke-shrouded mountain lay beyond the darkened bush. 'Mount Bundoon. You were so unfit.

It was mean of me to make you walk, but you wanted to come.'

'I only did it because I was besotted with you.'

'And I only made you come because I wanted you to see. Because I knew it was worth it. Because I knew you'd think it was worth it.' His hand was still holding hers, firm and strong. 'So you struggled up the track and I helped you…'

'You pushed. You bullied!'

'So I did and you got blisters on blisters and we hadn't taken enough water and we were idiots.'

'And then we reached the top,' she said, remembering.

'Yeah,' he said in satisfaction and hauled her against him. 'We reached the top and we looked out over the gorge and it's the most beautiful place in the whole world. Only gained through blisters.'

'Rob…'

'And what do you remember now?' he demanded, rough again. 'Blisters?'

'No.'

'So? Does my saying Aiden's name, Christopher's name, my name—does it hurt so much you can't reach the top? Because you know what I reckon, Jules? I reckon that saying Aiden's name and Christopher's, and talking of them to each other, that's the top. That's what we ought to aim for. If we could start loving the boys again…together…could we do that, Jules? Not just now? Not just for Christmas? For ever?'

And she wanted to. With every nerve in her body she wanted to.

'Do you know what I've done every Christmas?' he asked, gently now, holding her, but there was something implacable about his voice, something that said he was about to say something that would hurt. 'And every birthday. And so many times in between…I've taken that damned recording out and watched it. And you know what? I love it. I love that I have it. I love that my kids—and my Julie—can still make me smile.'

'You…you have it?' She was stammering. 'But tonight…I had to find the disc.'

'That's because tonight had to be your choice. I have a copy. Jules, I've made my choice. I'm living on, with my kids, with my memories and I've figured that's the way to survive. But you have to do your own figuring. Whether you want to continue blocking the past out for ever. Whether you want to let the memories back in. Or maybe…maybe whether you dare to move forward. With me or without. Julie, I still want you. You're still my wife. I still love you, but the rest…it's up to you.'

The night grew even more still. It was as if the world was holding its breath.

He was so close and he was holding her and he wanted her. All she had to do was sink into him and let him love her.

All she had to do was love in return.

But what did she have to give? It'd be all one way, she thought, her head spinning. Rob could say he loved her, he could say he still wanted her but it wasn't the Julie of now that he wanted. It was the Julie of years ago. The Julie she'd seen on replay. Today's Julie was like a husk, the shed skin of someone she had once been.

Rob deserved better.

She loved this man; she knew she did. But he deserved the old Julie and, confused or not, dizzy or not, she knew at some deep, basic level that she didn't have the energy to be that woman.

'Jules, you can,' he said urgently, as if he knew what she was thinking—how did he do that? How did he still have the skill?

How could she still know him when so much of her had died?

She wanted him, she ached for him, but it terrified her. Could she pretend to be the old Julie? she wondered. Could she fake being someone she used to be?

'Try for us,' Rob demanded, and his hands held her. He tugged her to him, and she felt…

like someone was hauling the floor from under her feet.

Rob would catch her. Rob would always catch her.

She had to learn to catch herself.

'Maybe I should see the same shrink,' she managed. 'The one who's made you brave enough to start again.'

'The shrink didn't make me brave. That's all me.'

'I don't want…'

'That's just it. You have to want. You have to want more than to hide.'

'You can't make me,' she said, almost resentfully, and he nodded.

'I know I can't. But the alternative? Do you want to walk away? Once the road is reopened, once Christmas is over, do you want to go back to the life you've been existing in? Not living, existing. Is that what you want?'

'It's what I have to want.'

'It's not,' he said, really angry now. 'You can change. Ask Danny. His Christmas list was written months ago. Amina said he wanted a bike but he got a wombat instead and you know what? Now he thinks that's what he wanted all along.'

'You think I can be happy with second best? Life without our boys?'

'I think you can be happy. I think dying with them is a bloody waste.'

'There's no need…'

'To swear? No, I suppose not. There's no need to do anything. There's no need to even try. Okay, Jules, I'll back off.'

'Rob, I'm…'

'Don't you dare say you're sorry. I couldn't bear it.'

But there was nothing to say but sorry so she said nothing at all. She stood and looked down at her feet. She listened to the soft scuffles of the wallabies out in the garden. She thought… she thought…

'Please?'

And the outside world broke in. The one word was a harsh plea, reverberating through the stillness and it came from neither of them. She turned and so did Rob.

Henry was in the open doorway, his hands held out in entreaty.

'Please,' he said again. 'Can either of you… do either of you know…?'

'What?' Rob said. 'Henry, what's wrong?'

'It's Amina,' Henry stammered. 'She says the baby's coming.'

CHAPTER EIGHT

ALL THE WAY to the bedroom Julie hoped Henry might be mistaken. They reached the guest room, however, and one look told her that there could be no mistake about this. Amina was crouched by the bed, holding onto the bed post, clinging as if drowning. She swung round as Julie entered and her eyes were filled with panic.

'It can't come. It's too early. I can't…last time it was so… I can't do this.'

Right. Okay.

'And it's breech,' Amina moaned. 'It was supposed to turn; otherwise the doctor said I might need a Caesarean…'

Breech! A baby coming and breech! Things that might best have been known when the fire crew was here, Julie thought wildly. They'd had that one chance to get away from here. If they'd known they could have insisted on help, on helicopter evacuation. Amina would surely have been a priority. But now…it was nine o'clock on Christmas night and they'd already knocked back help. What was the chance of a passing ambulance? Or a passing anything?

They were trapped. Their cars were stuck in the garage. The tree that had fallen over the driveway was still there, huge and smouldering. It had taken Henry almost twelve hours to walk up from the road blocks and he'd risked his life doing so.

'The phone…' she said without much hope, and Rob shook his head.

'I checked half an hour ago.' He rechecked then, flipping it from his pocket. 'No reception. Zip. Jules, I'll start down the mountain by foot. I might find someone with a car.'

'I didn't see an occupied house all the way up the mountain.' Henry shook his head. 'The homes that aren't burned are all evacuated. Amina, can't you stop?'

Amina said something that made them all blink. Apparently stopping was not on the agenda.

'What's wrong with Mama?' It was Danny, standing in the hall in his new Batman pyjamas. The pyjamas Julie had bought for her sons. The pyjamas that she'd thought would make her feel…make her feel…

But there wasn't time for her to feel anything. Danny's voice echoed his father's fear. Amina looked close to hysterics. Someone had to do something—now.

She was a lawyer, Julie thought wildly. She didn't do babies.

But it seemed she had no choice. By the look of Amina, this baby was coming, ready or not.

Breech.

'You'll be fine,' she said with a whole lot more assurance than she was feeling. 'Rob, take Danny into the living room and turn on a good loud movie. He had a nap this afternoon; he won't be sleepy. Isn't that right, Danny?'

'But what's wrong with Mama?'

She took a deep breath and squatted beside the little boy. Behind her, Henry was kneeling by his wife—remonstrating? For heaven's sake—as if Amina could switch anything off. And Danny looked terrified.

And suddenly Julie was done with terror. *Enough.*

'Danny, your mama is having a baby,' she told him. 'There's nothing to worry about. There's nothing wrong, but I suspect this is a big baby and your mama will hurt a bit as she pushes it out.'

'How will she push it out?'

'Rob will tell you,' she said grandly, 'while he finds a movie for you to watch. Won't you, Rob?'

'Um…yeah?' He looked wild-eyed and suddenly Julie was fighting an insane desire to grin. A woman in labour or teaching a kid the facts of life—what a choice.

'And your papa and I will help your mama,' she added. But…

'No.' It was Amina, staring up at them, practically yelling. 'No,' she managed again, and this time it was milder. 'It's okay, Danny,' she managed, making a supreme effort to sound normal in the face of her son's fear. 'This is what happened when I had you. It's normal. Having babies hurts, but only like pulling a big splinter out.' *As if,* Julie thought. *Right.*

'But Papa's not going to stay here.' Amina's voice firmed, becoming almost threatening, and she looked up at Julie and her eyes pleaded. 'Last time…Henry fainted. I was having Danny and suddenly the midwives were fussing over Henry because he cut his head on the floor when he fell. Henry, I love you but I don't want you here. I want you to go away.'

Which left…Julie and Rob. They met each other's gaze and Julie's chaotic thoughts were exactly mirrored in Rob's eyes.

Big breath. No, make that deep breathing. A bit of Zen calm. Where was a nice safe monastery when she needed one?

'Give us a moment,' she said to Amina.

'Henry, no fainting yet. Help Amina into bed, then you and Danny can leave the baby delivering to us. We can do this, can't we, Rob?'

'I...'

'*You* won't faint on me,' she said in a voice of steel.

'I guess I won't,' Rob managed. 'If you say so—I guess I wouldn't dare.'

She propelled him out into the passage and closed the door. They stared at each other in a moment of mutual panic, while each of them fought for composure.

'We can't do this,' Rob said.

'We don't have a choice.'

'I don't have the first clue...'

'I've read a bit.' And she had. When she was having the twins, the dot-point part of her—she was a lawyer and an accountant after all, and research was her thing—had read everything she could get her hands on about childbirth. The fact that she'd forgotten every word the moment she went into labour was immaterial. She knew it all. In theory.

'You're a lawyer, Jules,' Rob managed. 'Not an obstetrician. All you know is law.'

And she thought suddenly, fleetingly: *that's not all I have to be.*

Why was it a revelation?

Weirdly, she was remembering the day she'd got the marks to get into law school. Her hippy parents had been baffled, but Julie had been elated. From that moment she'd been a lawyer.

Even when the twins were born...she'd loved Rob to bits and she'd adored her boys but she was always a lawyer. She'd had Rob bring files into hospital after she'd delivered, so she wouldn't fall behind.

All you know is law...

For the last four years law had been her cave, her hiding place. Her all. The night the boys were killed they'd been running late because of her work and Rob's work.

Rob had started skiing, she thought inconsequentially and then she thought that maybe it was time she did something different too. Like delivering babies?

The whole concept took a nanosecond to wash through her mind but, strangely, it settled her.

'We don't even have the Internet,' Rob groaned.

'I have books.'

'Books?'

'You know: things with pages. I bought every birth book I could get my hands on when the twins were due. They'll still be in the bookcase.'

'You intend to deliver a breech baby with one hand while you hold the book in the other?'

'That's where you come in, Rob McDowell,' she snapped. 'From this moment we're a united team. I want hot water, warm towels and a professional attitude.'

'I'm an architect!'

'Not tonight you're not,' she told him. 'It's still Christmas. You played Santa this morning. Now you need to put your midwife hat on and deliver again.'

She'd sounded calm enough when she'd talked to Rob but, as she stood in front of her small library of childbirth books, she felt the calm slip away.

What...? How...?

Steady, she told herself. *Think.* She stared at the myriad titles and tried to decide.

Not for the first time in her life, she blessed her memory. Read it once, forget it never. Obviously she couldn't remember every detail in these books—some parts she'd skimmed over fast. But the thing with childbirth, she'd figured, was that almost anyone could do it. Women had been doing it since time immemorial and they'd done it without the help of books. Ninety-nine times out of a hundred there were no problems; all the midwife had to do was encourage, support, catch and clean up.

But the one per cent...

Julie had become just a trifle obsessive in the last weeks of her pregnancy. She therefore had books with pictures of unthinkable outcomes. She remembered Rob had found her staring in horror at a picture of conjoined twins, and a mother who'd laboured for days before dying. *Extreme Complications of Pregnancy.* He'd taken that book straight to the shredder, but she had others.

Breech, she thought frantically, fingering one title after another. There were all sorts of complications with breech deliveries and she'd read them all.

But…but…

Ninety-nine per cent of babies are born normally, she told herself and she kept on thinking of past reading. *Breech is more likely to be a problem in first time mothers because the perineum is unproven.* Or words to that effect? She'd read that somewhere and she remembered thinking if her firstborn twin was breech it might be a problem, but if the book was right the second twin would be a piece of cake regardless.

'You're smiling!'

Rob had come into the living room and was staring at her in astonishment.

'No problem. We can do this.' And she hauled out one of the slimmest tomes on the shelf, almost a booklet, written by a midwife and not a doctor. It was well thumbed. She'd read it over and over because in the end it had been the most comforting.

She flicked until she found what she was looking for, and there were the words again. *If the breech is a second baby it's much less likely to require intervention.* But it did sound a warning. *Avoid home birth unless you're near good medical backup.*

There wasn't a lot of backup here. One architect, one lawyer, one fainting engineer and a four-year-old. Plus a first aid box containing sticking plasters, tweezers and antiseptic.

Breech... She flipped to the page she was looking for and her eyes widened. Rob looked over her shoulder and she felt him stiffen. 'My God...'

'We can do this.' *Steady,* she told herself. *If I don't stay calm, who will?* 'Look,' she said. 'We have step by step instructions with pictures. It's just like buying a desk and assembling it at home, following instructions. Besides, if we need to intervene, we can, but it says we probably won't need to. It's big on hands off.'

'But if we do? You know me and kit furniture—it always ends up with screws left over and one side wonkier than the other. And look what it says! If it's facing upward, head for hospital because...'

'There's no need to think like that,' she snapped. 'We need to stay positive. That means calm, Rob.' And she thought back, remembering. 'Forget the kit furniture analogy. Yes, you're a terrible carpenter but as a first time dad you were great. You are great. You need to be like you were with me, every step of the way. No matter how terrified I was, you were there saying how brave I was, how well I was doing, and you sounded so calm, so sure...'

'I wasn't in the least sure. I was a mess.'

'So you're a good actor. Put the act on again.'

'This isn't you we're talking about. Jules, I could do it when I had to.'

'Then you have to now.' She took a long, hard look at the diagrams, committing them to memory. Hoping to heaven she wouldn't need them. 'Amina has us. Rob, together we can do this.'

'Okay.' He took a deep breath while he literally squared his shoulders. 'If you say so, maybe we can.' Then suddenly he tugged her to him and hugged her, hard, and gave her a swift firm kiss. 'Maybe that's what I've been saying all along. Apart we're floundering. Together we might...'

'Be able to have a baby? Do you have those

towels warming?' The kiss had left her flustered, but she regrouped fast.

'Yes, ma'am.'

'I'll need sterilised scissors.'

'I already thought of that. They're in a pot on the barbecue. So all we need is one baby.' He cupped her chin and smiled down at her. 'Okay, Dr McDowell, do you have your dot-point plan ready? I hope you do because we're in your hands.'

Breech births were supposed to be long. Weren't they? Surely they were supposed to take longer than normal labours, but no one seemed to have told Amina's baby that. When Rob and Julie returned to her room she was mid-contraction and one look at her told them both that this was some contraction. Surely a contraction shouldn't be as all-consuming if it was early labour.

Henry and Danny were looking appalled but Henry was looking even more appalled than his son. He'd fainted at Danny's birth, but then refugees did it tough, Rob thought, and who knew what the circumstances had been? Today he'd literally walked through fire to reach his family. He must be past exhaustion. He'd cut him some slack—and, besides, if Henry left with Danny, it would be Henry who'd have to explain childbirth to his son.

He put his hand on Henry's shoulder and gripped, hard.

'We can do this, mate,' he said. 'At least, Julie can and I'm here to assist. Julie suggested I take Danny into the living room and turn on a movie. If it's okay with Amina, how about you take my place? We have a pile of kids' movies. Pick a loud, exciting one and watch it until you both go to sleep. Hug Luka and know everything's okay. Danny, your mama's about to have a baby and she needs to be able to yell a bit while she does. It's okay, honest, most mamas yell when they have babies. So if you hear yelling, don't you worry. Snuggle up with your papa and Luka, and when you wake up in the morning I reckon your mama will have a baby to show you. Is that okay, Henry?'

'I'll stay,' Henry quavered. 'If you want me to, Amina…'

'Leave,' Amina ordered, easing back from the contraction enough to manage a weak smile at her husband and then her son. 'It's okay, sweetheart,' she told Danny. 'This baby has to push its way out and I have to squeeze and squeeze and it's easier for me if I can yell when I squeeze. Papa's going to show you a movie and Julie and Rob are going to stay with me to take care of the baby when it's born.'

'Can I come back and see it—when it's born?'

'Yes.'

'And will it be a boy?'

'I don't know,' Amina told him. 'But, Danny, take your papa away because I have to squeeze again and Papa doesn't like yelling. You look after Papa, okay?'

'And watch a movie?'

'Yes,' Amina managed through gritted teeth. Julie got behind Henry and practically propelled him and his son through the door and closed it behind them, and it was just as well because Amina was true to her word.

She yelled.

Hands off. Do not interfere unless you have to. That was the mantra the little book extolled and that was fine by Julie because there didn't seem to be an alternative.

She and Rob both washed, scrupulously on Julie's part, the way she'd seen it done on television. Rob looked at her with her arms held out, dripping, and gave a rueful chuckle. 'Waiting for a nurse to apply latex gloves?'

'The only gloves I have are the ones I use for the washing-up. I'm dripping dry,' she retorted and then another contraction hit and any thought of chuckling went out of the window.

'Hey,' Rob said, hauling a chair up by Amina's bedside. 'It's okay. Yell as much as you want.

We're used to it. You should have heard Julie when she had the twins. I'd imagine you could have heard her in Sri Lanka.'

'But…but she knows…what to do? Your Julie?'

'My Julie knows what to do,' Rob told her, taking her hand. 'My Julie's awesome.'

And how was a woman to react to that? Julie felt her eyes well, but then Rob went on.

'My Julie's also efficient. She'll help you get through this faster than anyone I know. And if there's any mucking around she'll know who to sue. She's a fearsome woman, my Julie, so let's just put ourselves in her hands, Amina, love, and get this baby born.'

Which meant there was no time for welling eyes, no time for emotion. There was a baby to deliver.

By unspoken agreement, Rob stayed by Amina's side and did what a more together Henry should have done, while Julie stayed at the business end of the bed.

The instructions in her little booklet played over and over in her head, giving her a clear plan of action. How close? Julie had no clue. She couldn't see the baby yet but, with the power of these contractions, it surely wouldn't be long before she did.

She felt useless, but at the other end of the bed Rob was a lot more help.

'Come on, Amina, you can do this. Every contraction brings your baby closer. You're being terrific. Did anyone ever teach you how to breathe? You do it like this between contractions…' And he proceeded to demonstrate puffing as he'd learned years before in Julie's antenatal classes. 'It really works. Julie said so.'

Julie had said no such thing, she thought. She'd said a whole lot of things during her long labour but she couldn't remember saying anything complimentary about anything.

And Amina was in a similar mood. When Rob waited until the next contraction passed and then encouraged Amina to puff again, he got told where he could put his puffing.

'And it's breech,' she gasped. 'Julie doesn't know about breech.'

'Julie knows everything,' Rob declared. 'Memory like a bull elephant, my Julie. Tell us the King of Spain in 1703, Jules.'

'Philip Five,' Julie said absently.

'Name a deadly mushroom?'

'Conocybe? Death caps? How many do you want?'

'And tell me what's different about breech?'

'I might have to do a little rotating as the baby

comes out,' Julie said, trying to sound as if it was no big deal.

'There you go, then,' Rob approved as Amina disappeared into another contraction. 'She knows it all. This'll be a piece of cake for our Julie.'

Only it wasn't. Rob had managed to calm Amina; there no longer seemed to be terror behind the pain, but there was certainly a fair bit of terror behind Julie's façade of competence.

One line in the little book stood out. *If the baby's presenting face up then there's no choice; it must be a Caesarean.*

Any minute now she'd know. *Dear God...*

Her mind was flying off at tangents as she waited. Was there any other option? They couldn't go for help. They couldn't ring anyone. For heaven's sake, they couldn't even light a fire and send out smoke signals. If it was face up...

'And my Julie always stays calm,' Rob said, and his voice was suddenly stern, cutting across the series of yelps Amina was making. 'That's what I love about her. That's why you're in such good hands, Amina. Are you sure you don't want to puff?'

Amina swore and slapped at his hand and a memory came back to Julie—she'd done exactly the same thing. She'd even bruised him. The day after the twins were born she'd looked at a blackening bruise on her husband's arm, and she'd also seen marks on his palm where her nails had dug in.

Her eyes met his and he smiled, a faint gentle smile that had her thinking…*memories can be good*. The remembrance of Rob's comfort. Her first sight of her babies.

The love…

Surely that love still deserved to live. Surely it shouldn't be put away for ever in the dusty recesses of her mind, locked away because letting it out hurt?

Surely Rob was right to relive those memories. To let them make him smile…

But then Amina gasped and struggled and Rob supported her as she tried to rise. She grasped her knees and she pushed.

Stage two. Stage two, stage two, stage two.

Face up, face down. *Please, please, please…*

There was a long, loaded pause and Amina actually puffed. But still she held her knees while the whole world seemed to hold its breath.

Another contraction. Another push.

Julie could see it. She could see…what? *What?*

A backside. A tiny bottom.

Face down. *Oh, God, face down. Thank you, thank you, thank you.* She glanced up at Rob and her relief must have shown in her face. He gave her a fast thumbs-up and then went back to holding, encouraging, being...Rob.

She loved him. She loved him with all her heart but now wasn't the time to get corny. Now was the time to try and deliver this baby.

Hands off. That was what the book said. *Breech babies will often deliver totally on their own.*

Please...

But they'd been lucky once. They couldn't ask for twice. Amina pushed, the baby's bottom slid out so far but as the contraction receded, so did the baby.

Over and over.

Exhaustion was starting to set in. Time for Dr Julie to take a hand? Did she dare?

Another glance at Rob, and his face was stern. He'd read the book over her shoulder, seen the pictures, figured what was expected now. His face said: *do it.*

So do it.

She'd set out what she'd need. Actually, she'd set out what she had. The book said if the head didn't come, then forceps might be required. She didn't actually have forceps or anything that could be usefully used instead.

Please don't let them be needed. It was a silent prayer said over and over.

Don't think forward. One step at a time. First she had to deliver the legs.

Dot-point number one. Carefully, she lubricated her fingers. One leg at a time. One leg…

Remember the pictures.

'Jules is about to help your baby out,' Rob said, his voice steady, calm, settling. 'Next push, Amina, go as far as you can and then hold. Puff, just like I said. Keep the pressure on.'

Next contraction… The baby's back slid out again. Deep breath and Julie felt along the tiny leg. What did the book say? *Manoeuvre your finger behind the knee and gently push upward. This causes the knee to flex. Hold the femur, splint it gently with your finger to prevent it breaking. This should allow the leg to…*

It did! It flopped out. *Oh, my…*

Calm. Next. Dot-point number two.

The other leg was easier. Now the baby could no longer recede. *Manoeuvre to the right position. Flex.*

Two legs delivered. She was almost delirious with hope. *Please…*

Dot-point number three. *Gently rotate the baby into the side position to allow delivery of the right arm.* Easier said than done but the illustrations had been clear. If only her hands weren't so slippery, but they had to be slippery.

'Fantastic, Jules,' Rob said. 'Fantastic, Amina. You're both doing great.'

She had the tiny body slightly rotated. Enough? It had to be. Her finger found the elbow, put her finger over the top, pressured gently, inexorably.

An arm. She'd delivered an arm. The dot-points were blurring, but she still had work to do. She was acting mostly on instinct, but thank God for the book. She'd write to the author. No, she'd send the author half her kingdom. All her kingdom.

She suddenly thought of the almost obscene amount of money she'd been earning these past years and thought...

And thought there was another arm to go and then the head, and the head was...

'Jules. We're doing great,' Rob growled and she glanced up at him and thought he'd seen the shiver of panic and he was grounding her again.

He'd always grounded her. She needed him.

Her hands held the tiny body, took a grip, lifted as the book said, thirty degrees so the left arm was in position for delivery. She twisted as the next contraction eased. The baby rotated like magic.

She found the elbow and pushed gently down. The left arm slithered out.

Now the head. *Please, God, the head.* She

didn't have forceps. She wouldn't have the first clue what to do with forceps if she had them.

'Lift,' Rob snapped and he was echoing the book too. 'Come on, Jules, you know what the book says. Come on, Amina. Our baby's so close. We can do this.'

Our baby…

It sounded good. It sounded right.

'Next contraction, puff afterwards, ease off until Jules has the baby in position,' Rob urged Amina, and magically she did.

Amina was working so hard. Surely she could do the same.

She steadied. Waited. The next contraction passed. Amina puffed, Rob held her hand and murmured gentle words. 'Hold, Amina, hold, we're so close…'

Do it.

She held the baby, resting it on her right hand. She manoeuvred her hand so two fingers were on the side of the tiny jaw. With her other hand she put her middle finger on the back of the baby's head.

It sounded easy. It wasn't. She lifted the baby as high as she could, remembering the pictures, remembering…

So much sweat. She needed…she needed…

'You're doing great, Jules,' Rob said. 'Amina, your baby's so close. Maybe one more push.

This is fantastic. Let's do this, people. Okay, Jules?'

'O…Okay.' She nodded. She'd forgotten how to breathe. *Please…*

'Okay, Amina, push,' Rob ordered and Amina pushed—and the next second Julie had a healthy, lusty, slippery bundle of baby girl in her arms.

She gasped and staggered but she had her. She had Amina's baby.

Safe. Delivered.

And seconds later a tiny girl was lying on her mother's tummy. Amina was sobbing with joy, and a new little life had begun.

After that things happened in a blur. Waiting for the afterbirth and checking it as the book had shown. Clearing up. Watching one tiny girl find her mother's breast. Ushering an awed and abashed Henry into the room, with Danny by his side.

Watching the happiness. Watching the little family cling. Watching the love and the pride, and then backing out into the night, their job done.

Julie reached the passage, leaned against the wall and sagged.

But she wasn't allowed to sag for long. Her husband had her in his arms. He held her and held her and held her, and she felt his heart beat against hers and she thought: *here is my home.*

Here is my family.

Here is my heart.

'Love, I need to check the boundaries again,' he said at last, ruefully, and she thought with a jolt: *fire.* She hadn't thought of the fire for hours. But of course he was right. There'd still be embers falling around them. They should have kept checking.

'We should have told Henry to check,' she managed.

'Do you think he would have even seen an ember? You take a shower. I'll be with you soon.'

'Rob…' she managed.

'Mmm?'

'I love you,' she whispered.

'I love you too, Dr McDowell.' He kissed her on the tip of the nose and then put her away. 'But then, I always have. All we need to do now is to figure some way forward. Think of it in the shower, my Jules. Think of me. Now, go get yourself clean again while I rid myself of my obstetric suit and put on my fireman's clothes. Figuring roles for ourselves… This day's thrown plenty at us. Think about it, Jules, love. What role do you want for the rest of your life?'

And he was gone, off to play fireman.

While Julie was left to think about it.

* * *

There was little to think about—and yet there was lots. She thought really fast while she let the water stream over her. Then she towelled dry, donned her robe and headed back out onto the veranda.

Rob was just finishing, heading up the steps with his bucket and mop.

'Not a single ember,' he announced triumphantly. 'Not a spark. After today I doubt an ember would dare come close. Have I told you recently that we rock? If I didn't think Amina might be asleep already I'd puff out my chest and do a yodel worthy of Tarzan.'

'Riiiight…'

'It's true. In fact I feel a yodel coming on right this minute. But not here. Do you fancy wandering up the hill a little and yodelling with me?'

And it was such a crazy idea that she thought: *why not?* But then, she was in a robe and slippers and she should…

No. She shouldn't think of reasons not to. *Move forward.*

'That's something I need to hear,' she said and grinned. 'A Tarzan yodel… Wow.' She grabbed his mop, tossed it aside, took his hand and hauled him out into the night.

'Jules! I didn't mean…'

'To yodel? Rob McDowell, if you think I'm

going through what we've gone through without listening to you yodel, you're very much mistaken.'

'What have I done?' But Rob was helpless in her hands as she hauled him round the back of the bunker, up through the rocks that formed the back of their property, along a burned out trail that led almost straight up—it was so rocky here that no trees grew, which made it safe from the remnants of fire—and out onto a rock platform where usually she could see almost all over the Blue Mountains.

She couldn't see the Blue Mountains tonight. The pall of smoke was still so thick she could hardly see the path, but the smoke was lifting a little. They could sometimes see a faint moon, with smoke drifting over, sending them from deep dark to a little sight and back again. It didn't matter, though. They weren't here to see the moon or the Blue Mountains. They were here…to yodel.

'Right,' Julie said as they reached the platform. 'Go ahead.'

'Really?'

'Was it all hot air? You never meant it?'

He chuckled. 'It won't be pretty.'

'I'm not interested in pretty!'

'Well, you asked for it.' And he breathed in, swelled, pummelled his chest—and yodelled.

It was a truly heroic yodel. It made Julie double with laughter. It made her feel...feel...as if she was thirteen years old again, in love for the first time and life was just beginning.

It was a true Tarzan yodel.

'You've practised,' she said accusingly. 'No one could make a yodel sound that good first try.'

'My therapist said I should let go my anger,' he told her. 'It started with standing in the shower and yelling at the soap. After a while I started experimenting elsewhere.'

'Moving on?'

'It's what you have to do.'

'Rob...'

'I know,' he said. 'You haven't. But you will. Try it yourself. Open your mouth and yell.' And he stood back and dared her with his eyes. He was laughing, with her, though, not at her. Daring her to laugh with him. Daring her to yodel?

And finally, amazingly, it felt as if she could. How long had it been since she'd felt this free? This alive? Maybe never. Even when they were courting, even when the twins were born, she'd always felt the constraints of work. The constraints of life. But now...

Rob's hands were exerting a gentle pressure but that pressure was no constraint. She was facing outward into the rest of the world.

She was facing outward into the rest of her life.

'Can you do it?' Rob asked, and he kissed the nape of her neck. 'Not that I doubt you. My wife can do anything.'

And she could. Or at least maybe she could.

Deep breath. Pummel a little.

Yodel.

And she was doing it, yodelling like a mad woman, and she took another breath and tried again and this time Rob joined her.

It was crazy. It was ridiculous.

It was fun.

'We've delivered a Christmas baby,' Rob managed as finally they ran out of puff, as finally they ran out of yodel. 'A new life. And we're learning Christmas yodelling duets! Is there nothing we're not capable of? Happy Christmas, Mrs McDowell, and, by the way, will you marry me? Again? Make our vows again? I know we're not divorced but it surely feels like we have been. Can we be a family? Can we take our past and live with it? Can we love what we've had, and love each other again for the rest of our lives?'

And the smoke suddenly cleared. Everything cleared. Rob was standing in front of her, he was holding her and the future was hers to grasp and to hold.

And in the end there was nothing to say except the most obvious response in the whole world.

'Why, yes, Mr McDowell,' she whispered. 'Happy Christmas, my love, and yes, I believe I will marry you again. I believe I will marry you—for ever.'

CHAPTER NINE

A RETAKING OF weddings vows shouldn't be as romantic as the first time around. That was what Julie's mother had read somewhere, but she watched her daughter marry for the second time and she thought: *what do 'they' know?*

People go into a second marriage with their eyes wide open, with all the knowledge of the trials and pitfalls of marriage behind them, and yet they choose to step forward again, and step forward with joy. Because they know what love is. Because they know that, despite the hassles and the day-to-day trivia, and sometimes despite the tragedy and the heartache, they know that love is worth it.

So Julie's mother held her husband's hand and watched her daughter retake her vows, and felt her heart swell with pride. They'd ached every step of the way with their daughter. They'd ached for their grandsons and for the hurt they'd known their son-in-law must be feeling. But in the end they'd stopped watching. Julie had driven them away, as she'd driven away most people in her life. But somehow one magical Christmas had brought healing.

It was almost Easter now. Julie had wanted to get on with their lives with no fuss, but Rob wasn't having any part of such a lame new beginning. 'I watch people have parties for their new homes,' he'd said. 'How much more important is this? We're having a party for our new lives.'

And they would be new lives. So much had changed.

They'd moved—Julie from her sterile apartment in Sydney, Rob from his bachelor pad in Adelaide—but they'd decided not to move back to the Blue Mountains. Amina and Henry were in desperate need of a house—*'and we need to move on,'* they'd told them.

Together they'd found a ramshackle weatherboard cottage on the beach just south of Sydney. They'd both abandoned their jobs for the duration and were tackling the house with energy and passion—if not skill. It might end up a bit wonky round the edges, but already it felt like home.

But... *Home. Home is where the heart is,* so somehow, some way, it felt right that their vows were being made back here. On the newly sprouting gardens around Amina and Henry's home in the Blue Mountains, where there was love in spades. Amina and Henry had been over-joyed when Rob and Julie had asked to have the ceremony here.

'Because your love brought us together again,' Julie had told Amina. 'You and Henry, with your courage and your love for each other.'

'You were together all the time,' Amina had whispered, holding her baby daughter close. 'You just didn't know it.'

Rob and Julie were now godparents. More. They were landlords and they were also spon-soring Henry through retraining. There'd be no more working in the mines. No more long ab-sences. This family deserved to stay together.

As did Julie and Rob.

'I asked you this seven years ago,' the cel-ebrant said, smiling mistily at them. She must have seen hundreds of weddings, but did she mist up for all of them? Surely not. 'But I can't tell you the joy it gives me to ask you again. Rob, do you take Julie—again—to be your lawful wedded wife, to love and to cherish, in sickness and in health, forsaking all others, for as long as you both shall live?'

'I do—and the rest,' Rob said softly, speak-ing to Julie and to Julie alone. 'Beyond the grave I'll love you. Love doesn't end with death. We both know that. Love keeps going and going and going, if only we let it. Will we let it? Will we let it, my love?'

'Yes, please,' Julie whispered, and then she, too, made her vows.

And Mr McDowell married Mrs McDowell—again—and the thing was done.

Christmas morning.

Julie woke early and listened to the sounds of the surf just below the house. She loved this time of day. Once upon a time she'd listened to galahs and cockatoos in the bush around their house. Now she listened to the sounds of the waves and the sandpipers and oystercatchers calling to each other as they hunted on the shore of a receding tide.

Only that wasn't right, she told herself. She'd never lain in bed and listened to the sounds of birds in the bush. She'd been too busy working. Too busy with her dot-points.

But now… They'd slowed, almost to a crawl. Her dot-points had grown fewer and fewer. Rob worked from home, his gorgeous house plans sprawled over his massive study at the rear of the house. Julie commuted to Sydney twice a week, and she, too, worked the rest of the time at home.

But they didn't work so much that they

couldn't lie in bed and listen to the surf. And love each other. And start again.

She'd stop commuting soon, she thought in satisfaction. She could maybe still accept a little contract work, as long as it didn't mess with her life. With her love.

With her loves?

And, unbidden, her hand crept to her tummy, where her secret lay.

She couldn't wait a moment longer. She rolled over and kissed her husband, tenderly but firmly.

'Wake up,' she told him. 'It's Christmas.'

'So it is.' He woke with laughter, reaching for her, holding her, kissing her. 'Happy Christmas, wife.'

'Happy Christmas, husband.'

'I have the best Christmas gift for you,' he said, pushing himself up so he was smiling down at her with all the tenderness in the world. 'I bet you can't guess what it is.'

She choked on laughter. Last night he'd driven home late and on the roof rack of his car was a luridly wrapped Christmas present, complete with a huge Christmas bow. It was magnificently wrapped but all the wrapping in the world couldn't disguise the fact that it was a surfboard.

'I have no idea,' she lied. 'I can't wait.'

They'd come so far, she thought, as Rob gathered her into his arms. This year would be so different from the past. All their assorted family was coming for lunch, as were Amina and Henry and their children. For family came in all sorts of assorted sizes and shapes. It changed. Tragedies happened but so did joys. Christmas was full of memories, and each memory was to be treasured, used to shape the future with love and with hope and memories to come.

And dot-points, she thought suddenly. There were—what?—twenty people due for lunch. Loving aside, smugness aside, she had to get organised. Dot-point number one. Stuff the turkey.

But Rob was holding her—and she had her gift for him.

So: *soon*, she told her dot-point, and proceeded to indulge her husband. And herself.

'Do you want your present now?' she asked as they finally resurfaced, though she couldn't get her mind to be practical quite yet.

'I have everything I need right here.'

'Are you sure?'

'What more could a man want?'

She smiled. She smiled and she smiled. She'd been holding this secret for almost two weeks and it had almost killed her not to tell him, but now... She tugged away from his arms, then kissed him on the nose and settled on her back. And tugged his hand to her naked tummy.

She could scarcely feel it herself. Could he…? Would he…?

But he got it in one. She saw his eyes widen in shock. He was clever, her husband. He was loving and tender and wise. He was a terrible handyman—her kitchen shelves were a disaster and she was hoping her dad might stay on long enough to fix them—but a woman couldn't have everything.

Actually, she did. She did have everything. Her husband was looking down at her with awe and tenderness and love.

'Really?' he whispered.

'Really.'

And she saw him melt, just like that. A blaze of joy that took her breath away.

Joy… They had so much, and this baby was more. For it was true what they said: *love doesn't die*. The memories of Christopher and Aiden would stay with them for ever—tender, joyous, always mourned but an intrinsic part of her family. Their family. Hers and Rob's.

'Happy Christmas, Daddy,' she murmured and she kissed him long and hard. 'Happy Christmas, my love.'

'Do you suppose it might be twins again?' he breathed, awed beyond belief, and she smiled and smiled.

'Who knows? Whoever it is, we'll love them

for ever. Like I love you. Now, are you going to make love to me again or are you going to let me go? I hate to mention it but I have all these dot-points to attend to.'

'But here is your number one dot-point,' he said smugly, and gathered her into his arms yet again. 'The turkey can wait. Christmas can wait. Number one is us.'

* * * * *

HARLEQUIN®

Romance

Available January 6, 2015

#4455 TAMING THE FRENCH TYCOON
by Rebecca Winters
Brooding tycoon Luc Charriere doesn't trust easily, but when it comes to beautiful CEO Jasmine Martin, he'll risk *everything* to keep the woman who stole his heart by his side...

#4456 HIS VERY CONVENIENT BRIDE
by Sophie Pembroke
Stepping into her sister's place at the altar beside gorgeous tycoon Flynn Ashton, dare Helena Morrison dream that this convenient marriage could be the fresh start they've both been hoping for?

#4457 THE HEIR'S UNEXPECTED RETURN
by Jackie Braun
The connection pretty Brigit Wright feels with new boss and notorious playboy Kellen Faust terrifies her—should she trust the renegade Faust heir to stay by her side...forever?

#4458 THE PRINCE SHE NEVER FORGOT
by Scarlet Wilson
Ruby Wetherspoon has never been far from Crown Prince Alexander's thoughts, but his duty to his country kept him away. Now he has the chance to make *both* their dreams come true!

HRLPCNM1214

LARGER-PRINT BOOKS!
GET 2 FREE LARGER-PRINT NOVELS PLUS
2 FREE GIFTS!

HARLEQUIN®

Romance

From the Heart, For the Heart

YES! Please send me 2 FREE LARGER-PRINT Harlequin® Romance novels and my 2 FREE gifts (gifts are worth about $10). After receiving them, if I don't wish to receive any more books, I can return the shipping statement marked "cancel." If I don't cancel, I will receive 4 brand-new novels every month and be billed just $4.84 per book in the U.S. or $5.24 per book in Canada. That's a savings of at least 19% off the cover price! It's quite a bargain! Shipping and handling is just 50¢ per book in the U.S. and 75¢ per book in Canada.* I understand that accepting the 2 free books and gifts places me under no obligation to buy anything. I can always return a shipment and cancel at any time. Even if I never buy another book, the two free books and gifts are mine to keep forever.

119/319 HDN F43Y

Name _____ (PLEASE PRINT)

Address _____ Apt. #

City _____ State/Prov. _____ Zip/Postal Code

Signature (if under 18, a parent or guardian must sign)

Mail to the **Harlequin® Reader Service:**
IN U.S.A.: P.O. Box 1867, Buffalo, NY 14240-1867
IN CANADA: P.O. Box 609, Fort Erie, Ontario L2A 5X3
Want to try two free books from another line?
Call 1-800-873-8635 or visit www.ReaderService.com.

* Terms and prices subject to change without notice. Prices do not include applicable taxes. Sales tax applicable in N.Y. Canadian residents will be charged applicable taxes. Offer not valid in Quebec. This offer is limited to one order per household. Not valid for current subscribers to Harlequin Romance Larger-Print books. All orders subject to credit approval. Credit or debit balances in a customer's account(s) may be offset by any other outstanding balance owed by or to the customer. Please allow 4 to 6 weeks for delivery. Offer available while quantities last.

Your Privacy—The Harlequin® Reader Service is committed to protecting your privacy. Our Privacy Policy is available online at www.ReaderService.com or upon request from the Harlequin Reader Service.

We make a portion of our mailing list available to reputable third parties that offer products we believe may interest you. If you prefer that we not exchange your name with third parties, or if you wish to clarify or modify your communication preferences, please visit us at www.ReaderService.com/consumerchoice or write to us at Harlequin Reader Service Preference Service, P.O. Box 9062, Buffalo, NY 14269. Include your complete name and address.

THIS TIME SHE searched for his mouth with stunning
impatience, telling him without words. Their kiss went on
and on until he felt transported.

But a different kind of pain than he'd known before shot
through him because this was her goodbye kiss. He pulled
her right up against his chest and buried his face in her neck.
She really was going away. This wasn't something he could
talk her out of.

"Jasmine? Before you leave for the States, I have to
spend some time with you. I'll take my vacation now. How
soon do you have to go?"

"I promised to be home on August 7. It's my parents'
thirtieth wedding anniversary party."

So soon? Everything in him rebelled. His mind calculated
the time. "That gives us a week."

A moan sounded before she moved off his lap and stood
up. "No more make believe, Luc. I couldn't go anywhere
with you."

He stared up at her. "Why not?"

"You *know* why. Your life is here. Mine is on the other
side of the Atlantic. How could it possibly be good for
either of us to go off for that long, knowing we're going to
say goodbye at the end? The thought of it is too painful to

even contemplate." Her voice throbbed. "At least it is for me. But you're a man, so it's different for you."

"Explain that remark."

Jasmine wouldn't look at him. "You can go away with a woman and enjoy the time thoroughly. When it's over you can move on. But women are different. Not all, but some. *I'm* different. To travel and make love with you, only to get on a plane at the end of that journey and wave goodbye sounds like a kind of purgatory I have no desire to live through."

He grasped her hand. "Then we won't sleep together."

She looked down at him and smiled. "You're a Frenchman aren't you?"

"I'm a man like all other men, and the thought of making love to you has been on my mind since I saw you on Yeronisos. But that isn't why I want to go away with you. If you think making love to you is all I'm after, then you have an odd conception about me.

"The other day I told you I have feelings for you I've never had for another woman. If all I can do is hold you and kiss you while we're on vacation, it will be enough. What I'd truly regret is not being able to get to know Jasmine Martin, the fabulous woman inside the girl who makes me want to be a better man."

Don't miss
TAMING THE FRENCH TYCOON
by Rebecca Winters,
available in January 2015 wherever
Harlequin® Romance books and ebooks are sold!

HREXP1214